I0600803

# Caly's Game

*Book One of The Sanctum Series*

## Trinity

http://www.TrinityWrites.com/

**Caly's Game**
**Copyright © 2018, 2015 by Trinity**

WriterTrinity@gmail.com

First e-Book Printing, 2015 by Loose Id, LLC

Image/art disclaimer: Licensed material is being used for illustrative purposes only. Any person depicted in the licensed material is a model.

ISBN : 978-0-9910778-6-1 (eBook)
ISBN : 978-0-9910778-7-8 (Print)
Editor: Rory Olsen
Cover Artist: Scott Carpenter
Published in the United States of America

This book is a work of fiction. While reference might be made to actual historical events or existing locations, the names, characters, places and incidents are either the product of the author's imagination or are used fictitiously, and any resemblance to actual persons, living or dead, business establishments, events, or locales is entirely coincidental.

## Warning

This book contains sexually explicit scenes and adult language and may be considered offensive to some readers.

-→➤➤◄◄←-

DISCLAIMER: Please do not try any new sexual practice, especially those that might be found in these BDSM/fetish titles without the guidance of an experienced practitioner. Author will not be responsible for any loss, harm, injury or death resulting from use of the information contained in any of her titles.

# Dedication

*I dedicate this book to my husband, who is my muse and my biggest supporter (even when he's telling me that my writing sucks — maybe especially then!) and also to J, who knows why.*

# Acknowledgment

*I'd be remiss if I didn't take the time to thank my beta reader, Linda Mercury, without whom there wouldn't have been a hot sex scene at the beginning and also without whom Caly would have been a little more uptight. Also, many, many thanks to the Atlanta BDSM community for their unending support of me in all my endeavors from being an author to being a kink educator and lots in between. As a reader, if you're interested in exploring kink a bit in real time and are located in or around the ATL, definitely check out the scene. You won't regret it.*

*And finally, all my gratitude to my most amazing editor, Rory Olsen, for helping me fill in my weak spots and make this manuscript great!*

# Chapter One

Being fat has kept me from doing some things in my life. Fucking is not one of them.

*Men are pretty easy, in general. Even the best-looking of them — guys some folks think are out of a fat girl's "league" — are easy. And they're always surprised when they're approached directly. Some of the looks I've gotten have almost made me laugh. Apparently most women are not particularly forward. The thing is…men love forward women.*

On the table, my phone vibrated with a text just as I finished typing. I made eye contact for the third time with a pretty hot bear-type guy at the bar. Friday nights were often my best nights. A blond—not my usual look—but with gorgeous green eyes that had caught my attention as soon as I walked into Chemistry, my home bar. He'd been nursing the same Heineken for the last twenty minutes, so not a drunk. Always a plus. I was about to flag down Sandy, my waitress, but the phone.

*Tessa: Where are you?*

*Me: Chemistry. It's been a long week. Need some companionship.*

*Tessa: You could have come over.*

*Me: Not that kind of companionship. :p*

*Tessa: Ah. Speaking of, how about dinner Sunday?*

*Me: Are you going to try to set me up again?*

*Tessa: No.*

*Me: Uh-huh. Who else is coming?*

*Tessa: Just a friend of Gordon's.*

*Me: Ugh.*

*Tessa: Don't be that way. He's a nice guy.*

Before I could even start my response, a shadow fell over the table. And there was Heineken-man, with a smile on his face and a lemon-drop martini in his hand.

"Hey. You look like you need a refill." He nodded to my empty glass. He had a nice voice. Just deep enough to let me imagine it growling in my ear, but not so deep that I couldn't hear him over the bar music. A fresh drink and a nice voice. Two points in his favor. But then there was the lost hunt. One point down for approaching.

"Looks that way. Thanks." I returned his smile while I debated whether it would be worth continuing the conversation. I always feel let down when the guy does the chasing. He was good-looking, yes, but I'm the one who does the hunting. Not the other way around. My phone buzzed again, and I ignored it. Tessa could wait awhile. I had more important issues at hand.

Heineken-man set the martini down—without spilling, which was to his credit. "May I join you?"

Very polite. There's a point. I still hadn't decided whether I wanted him to join me, though.

"If you're too busy"—my laptop was still open—"I understand." His eyes twinkled. Or maybe it was just the strobe light from the small dance floor behind my table. "I'd be disappointed, but I'd understand."

*Guh.* He was putting the moves on me. That was my job.

*Dammit, again.*

I supposed we could see where it went. No harm in that, right? "Sure. Have a seat." I closed the lid of my laptop and slid the machine into my satchel as he slid his nice derriere onto the bench seat across from me. Then, the martini. Sugar on the rim clashed very nicely with the tart lemon. I gazed at him over my glass. "Thank you for the drink."

"My pleasure. I'm Gary."

"Caly. It's nice to meet you. I don't think I've seen you here before."

"I'm not actually from around here. My sister lives in the neighborhood, and we had dinner tonight. I thought I'd stop in and check the place out. It seems nice enough." Up close, the green of his eyes was spectacular, a deep kelly green rimmed in hazel. I probably could have just stared at them for an hour. "You're a regular?"

"I come in once or twice a week, maybe, for a nightcap. Or to do some writing." I'd been working on the *How to Pick Up Dudes* book for a month or two.

Gary's eyebrows went up, as did the corners of his mouth. "A writer? What do you write?"

"Call it a self-help book. I'm not really a writer. I do it in my spare time." I took another sip of my drink. "You've got gorgeous eyes."

He laughed—an attractive laugh. Not one of those obnoxious guffaws that some bigger guys have. "Thank you. Aren't I supposed to be complimenting you?"

I shot my feistiest grin at him. "Well, you haven't yet, have you?"

He put a large hand on his chest, fingers splayed wide. "I am remiss in my duties! My deepest apologies." Okay, he was funny. And charming. I admire both of those things. "Would you like to know what drew me over here with a tangy drink sporting a sugar rim?"

"What?"

His eyes twinkled again in the low bar light. "The way you bite your lower lip when you're typing. It's pretty adorable."

It was my turn to laugh. This was going to turn out okay.

---

I kept my hands to myself long enough to let him in, close the door behind us, and drop my satchel onto a kitchen chair. It'd been three weeks since my last hunt. I was ready.

"This is a nice place—"

I shut him up with the press of my lips against his. He seemed startled for a moment, but then he bent, slid his arms around me, and pulled me against his solid chest. His warmth encompassed me as his tongue brushed my lower lip. I let him wait while I ran my hands along his shoulders, to his neck. He was way taller than me—I was up on my tiptoes.

His lips met mine again, his tongue put away for the time being. I started on the buttons of his shirt. He took that as his cue, and his hands skimmed my back, beneath my flowy blouse and tank top. Soon I was enveloped in his masculine smell, a mix of something woody and the Heineken he'd drunk. It suited him and only made him sexier. Desire pooled in my belly.

When we broke the kiss, his breath whooshed across my cheek, hot and sweet. "You're wearing too many clothes," he said, working my tank top up.

"Two layers. Blouse first, then the rest." I pushed his hands and stripped away the gauzy top. Then I went back to his shirt and finished unfastening the buttons. "We're both wearing too many clothes."

After some finagling, he got my tank off and I got his oxford off. Thick blond hair carpeted his broad chest and part of his belly. I ran my fingers through it, letting the coarseness tickle my skin. I smiled at him, and those green eyes caught me up again.

He reached behind me and popped my bra open with no trouble at all. My breasts tumbled free, and he threw my pretty cream-colored lace bra onto the floor.

Another whoosh of breath came from him. I didn't know whether it was surprise or appreciation—until he dropped to a crouch and lifted both breasts in his hands. Definitely appreciation. His hands were large and darkly tanned against the paleness of my breasts. He stared at them for a long moment. My skin tingled with my anticipation.

When he finally leaned forward and took my right nipple into his mouth, it was my turn to gasp. His mouth, hot and wet, sucked my nipple in, and his tongue went to work on the tip while it was inside. Little electric shocks went straight to my pussy. I breathed out a moan and let my eyes flutter shut.

After several moments, he released my nipple and then turned his attention to the other. This time, he used the tip of his tongue to flick and lick at my nipple. The cool air on my now wet nipple sent a shiver right up my spine.

I groaned, and my heart raced. I needed this man in the bedroom. I put my hands on his forearms. "Come on." I pulled away from him just enough for him to get the message. He rose, and I led the way, quickly, down the short hall to my bedroom.

Before we were even through the door, my hands were on his jeans. I managed the button with no trouble. I fumbled with the zipper. Why are those stupid zipper tabs so small? He didn't seem to mind—his hands stayed busy kneading my breasts. His thumbs occasionally brushed over my already sensitive nipples, which didn't help my zipper concentration at *all*.

He leaned in and kissed me, splitting that concentration even more and—wouldn't you know it— down came the zipper. I slid my hand into his jeans. His cock strained against the cotton of his underwear, hot and thick.

I love that part. The feeling of a hard cock before it's fully free. There's something so incredibly hot about the outline of it, running my nails over its length through the fabric. *God.*

I squeezed his cock, and his hips jerked toward me. I got satisfaction out of that. He grunted and then grabbed me by my forearms and half pushed, half walked me backward to the bed. We continued the kiss the whole way, lips bumping together, the taste of beer on my tongue. My calves hit the mattress, and we toppled onto it. His body covered mine, and he settled between my legs, hiking my skirt up my hips.

He broke the kiss long enough to say, "Condoms?"

"Drawer." I pointed to the nightstand.

He slid the drawer open and pulled out a foil square. As he tore it open with his teeth, he waggled his eyebrows at me. I laughed.

"What do you say, Caly? A down-and-dirty fuck with half our clothes on?" He hiked his briefs down and rolled the condom on as I looked down our bodies. His cock, tall and thick, stood out from a thatch of dark blond hair.

"Mmm. Yeah. That sounds good to me." I wrapped a leg around his as I watched him seat the condom.

Gary fell forward, arms on either side of me to hold himself up just above my body. His cock nestled my panty-clad pussy. The heat pulsed against me. He rocked his hips, and the head of his cock scraped against my clit, sending a hot sizzle through me. I arched my back, and he sucked a nipple into his mouth. The added sensation piled on top of the sizzle and brought it to a burn, flaming just beneath my skin. I ground my hips against him as my breath came in small gasps and pants.

I reached down between us and palmed his cock for a moment. Gary jerked his gaze up to mine, and my nipple slipped from his mouth. He groaned as I squeezed. His eyes shut. Then I hooked a finger on the edge of my panties and pulled them aside. I angled my hips until I felt the head of his cock nudging my entrance. Those green eyes opened again, and I gave him half a nod. "Come on. Fuck me."

That twinkle flashed through his eyes again, and he grinned. He eased his cock into me, slowly, inch by inch, and he watched me the whole time. He was thick and long, and my pussy stretched as he pushed, filling me with a feeling of delicious pleasure. I wrapped my legs around him. He leaned down and captured my lips with his just as he pushed the final way in. I shivered, tingles racing all along my body. I stabbed my tongue into his mouth and held him tight to me.

He grabbed one breast and squeezed it just before he pulled back almost completely. His lips left mine, and his gaze caught me again as he rammed home. The strength of him shuddered straight through me and a cry tore from my throat. He started fucking me fast and hard, and I couldn't catch my breath with the way his pelvis jammed into my clit with every thrust. Tingles turned to blossoms that shifted to a rising tide that began in my belly and pressed out to all my limbs. He never slowed, his cock rocketing in and out.

"I...I'm going to come," I said in between gasps. I couldn't believe it was happening this fast. I scrabbled at his arms that framed me, his muscles taut beneath my fingers.

"Do it. Come." His face, red with exertion, was set with a hard look of concentration, and I wondered for just a moment if he was holding back his orgasm. A moment to wonder was all I had.

The dam inside me finally broke, and everything went white-hot as raw feeling rushed through me. Electricity coursed along my skin and burst into my limbs. It overtook me and I let myself ride the wave until it ebbed to a ripple. Just as I all but collapsed under him, Gary let out a low howl and slammed into me twice more, his entire body shuddering over me. Sweat dripped onto my breasts.

Finally, he lowered himself and lay on me, his head nestled beside my ear. We both panted, chests heaving against each other. I closed my eyes and listened to the hammer of my heart slowing moment by moment.

"God," he whispered, his breath hot against my cheek. "You're a damn good fuck."

---

Gary had been a bit put out that I wouldn't let him stay the night, but overall was a good sport. He gave me his number, which I was fine with. He was a pretty good lay, after all. Whether I actually contacted him or not…well, that would be up for debate.

Friday was pretty relaxed in the office. We'd had a tangled litigation hearing earlier in the week that had gotten continued, but we were up to our eyeballs in taking depositions. I'd spent all day Wednesday and Thursday interviewing geeks and office admins from a tech company. Friday, my team vowed we were not even looking at the case again until Monday. It was really a pipe dream, and we all knew it. But it made Friday more low-key.

In the hedonism of the night with Gary, I'd completely forgotten about Tessa's dinner invitation for Sunday. That is, until it was almost quitting time and Tessa blew up my phone.

*Tessa: So?*

*Me: So what?*

*Tessa: Sunday. Dinner. You have no memory, do you? I should probably talk to your doctor about early senility.*

*Me: Shut up. I was otherwise engaged for the evening :p*

*Tessa: I'm sure. So are you coming or not? I mean dinner. Not other engagements.*

*Me: *laugh* Yeah, yeah, I'll be there.*

*Tessa: Good! I can't wait for you to meet Gordon's friend!*

*Me: Ugh.*

*Tess: Oh stop. What are you doing tonight?*

*Me: I've got that big formal thing tomorrow night, so I'm going to chill tonight. Probably hit Chemistry for a drink and some writing.*

*Tessa: You could come over.*

*Me: Nah. I've got a new section to write about how not to give out your phone number to guys you pick up, so they don't make you crazy.*

*Tessa: You're weird.*

*Me: I know. See you Sunday!*

*Tessa: Love you!*

*Me: You too :)*

---

I was still pretty sated from last night, so I really did spend most of the evening writing. A couple guys came by to chat, and one bought me a drink from across the room, but mostly I kept my nose in the screen.

Tessa might have thought I was a bit off, but I don't like giving my number out to guys I pick up. They've been taught by society that they're supposed to call or whatever within a certain amount of time from a date. But what I do isn't dating. It's fucking. And I don't want calls or texts from most of them. Some, yes, maybe. Mostly not, though. The point is, I want to be the one to choose. So sometimes it's a challenge figuring out how to keep my digits out of their phones.

Last night, I'd had to redirect the conversation twice while I was shooing Gary out of the apartment. In the end, I'd almost managed to avoid the whole phone-number conversation in all its glory; it was a close thing for a while. Gary was nice. He was pretty sexy. And he definitely knew how to use his cock. But I didn't want an attachment. I just wanted a fuck.

I'd wondered whether he'd show up at Chemistry again, but so far, I hadn't spotted his gorgeous green eyes. My libido was a bit disappointed, but my rational brain was happy with it.

Having almost finished the chapter I was working on, I had another scope around the bar. Out of habit, I surveyed the men. Most guys were paired up with a woman. One single guy in a blue work-shirt at the bar, a huge beer mug in front of him. Two guys in business casual watching a game on the television. One man in a business suit, tie loose, sitting alone at a small table, sipping on a short glass of probably bourbon or something. None of them really my type. Not that I was actively looking. But there's never anything wrong with passively looking, right?

I wrote a few more lines, halfheartedly, and then finished my martini. Nice and tart, just the way I like them. I left money for my check and a good tip for Sandy, then packed up my laptop.

I scanned the bar again as I slid into my light jacket. Not much change. A group of college-age girls with a couple frat boys in tow. Two more guys joined the ones watching the game. Things would get a lot busier as Friday evening wore on. Mr. Bourbon still sat with his loosened tie, though he was watching me. I flashed him a grin, slid out of the booth, and heaved my laptop bag onto my shoulder. He tilted his glass to me and gave a very slight nod.

*Hmmm.* Perhaps the Universe had a different plan for me tonight. I did a quick assessment of him. Black hair, cut high and tight. Former military? His broad shoulders and solid-looking chest could have meant he'd served. Olive skin, brown eyes, thick eyebrows. He looked comfortable in the suit, though, and not a lot of military guys liked the civilian uniform. He looked bulky but not huge.

*What the hell?* Couldn't hurt to try. At the very least, it might lay some groundwork for some fun in the future.

I weaved my way through the scattered tables, skirting the game table just as one of the guys jumped up and cheered a touchdown. Or something. Mr. Bourbon watched me approach, one corner of his mouth angled up only a tiny bit.

All right—challenge accepted.

I dropped my satchel into the chair across the table from him and dropped myself into the one to his right. His eyebrows lifted and maybe the curve of his mouth rose just a hair, but he said nothing. He raised his glass and took a small sip, watching me over the rim.

"Did you just move in?" I leaned back in the chair and smoothed my skirt. I'd come straight from work, so I looked presentable, at least. That's always important when hunting. Not that I'd been planning on hunting. But apparently now I was.

"Excuse me?" The almost-smirk hadn't left his face. He didn't look like he really cared whether I answered his question or not.

"Neighborhood bar. Haven't seen you here before. Assumed you're new to the neighborhood."

"Ahh." His gaze shifted to the getting-more-crowded-by-the-minute room, and he scanned it for a moment before swinging back to me. "Astute. Yes, I've bought a house a block and a half away."

"Welcome, then, Mr....?"

A beat before he answered. "Morrell. Evan Morrell." He didn't offer his hand.

"It's nice to meet you. I'm Caly Arling."

"A pleasure, Ms. Arling."

By now, most guys are clueing in to the fact that I might be available for some mutual fun-time. I didn't really need it tonight, but I could probably have been pretty easily persuaded. If Evan Morrell *had* clued in to it, he didn't let on. Maybe he was gay. That would explain it. Maybe fat girls repulsed him. That's okay too, I guess. Would rather know now than when I'm in bed with him. That's always awkward.

"And are you the neighborhood welcoming committee?" He didn't put any snarky tone to it or even innuendo. But it seemed like there was innuendo there anyway. I started feeling a little off my footing.

Normally, this would be where I'd close the deal—this would have been an easy one—except he still wasn't acting normal. I couldn't even be sure if he was trying to close the deal or not.

"Not really. I was just on my way out, and you seemed as if you might like a friendly face."

"Thank you," he said. "That was very kind." His eyes, a deep, solid brown, remained trained on me.

*Now what? This isn't going right. It's weird.* "Well, I'll leave you to your drink. Welcome and all that." I rose, no longer looking him in the face, and gathered my laptop. I slung the bag into my shoulder and turned away.

"Ms. Arling." When I looked back, he had an actual smile on his face. And it made a little dimple on his left cheek. Not both. Just his left. "I'm sure we'll see each other again."

Was he being creepy? I couldn't tell.

He raised his glass just a smidge. "Neighborhood bar and all."

I don't like being flustered. No, really. I *hate* being flustered. And Evan Morrell flustered the fuck out of me. I didn't like it. Not at all.

When I got home, I tossed my keys on the table by the door and almost threw my satchel onto the chair beside it. I hadn't even been looking for a fuck. Why did I feel like I'd just been shot down?

*Dammit. Stupid Evan Morrell.*

I changed into pajamas—yoga pants and a tank top— and settled in front of my real laptop. The one I did real work on. While most of my workday revolved around contract negotiations, occasionally something works out badly and we have to take a dispute to a mediator or a judge. I was just in the middle of one of those now and had a deposition on Monday. Since I was already in an arguing frame of mind, drafting questions seemed like a good thing to do.

---

My Saturdays are usually full with volunteering and sometimes hanging out with friends during the day, but I'd decided a few weeks ago to take a lazy weekend for myself. It coincided pretty well with the Friday morning vow at the office. I'd spent the morning at a day spa, getting a massage and having all the girlie things done to my fingers and toes. Another thing I don't do often, but it's nice now and again.

I'd tried not to think of Evan Morrell, but going to a spa by yourself means spending a lot of time in your own head.

By the time evening had rolled around, I'd gotten sick of thinking about him. As I got ready for the formal cocktail party my firm was throwing as a benefit for the homeless shelter Helping Hands, I resolved to put him out of my mind. I'd focus tonight on seeing if there was anyone worth a romp. It was rare that I hunted anywhere near a work function, but there would be more than enough folks so that it would probably be easy to find someone not associated with the firm itself.

For about eight seconds while I put on my makeup, I wished I'd thought to arrange a date for the evening. It might be nice to have someone on my arm—or be on his arm, more accurately, I suppose—for once. People were used to me going stag, though, so it's probably best to just live up to expectations.

I thought briefly about Gary. He would make a pretty sidearm. Ultimately I decided against it. It was easier on my own anyway, at the end of the night. No entanglements. No awkward good-byes when I didn't want to take him to bed.

I slid the dress up my body, then did the always graceful side-zipper-grapple. Some of the ways women's clothes are put together is annoying. But a side zip is probably better than a back zip for a single girl. It was a great dress too. Dark sapphire satin, floor length with a little bit of a fishtail at the bottom. Strapless, with a low-cut sweetheart neckline and a few tastefully placed rhinestones along the edge to show off the girls. A matching satin stole was the only nod to my insecurities about my flabby upper arms. I could wrap it around me when I was feeling particularly freaked out about them.

I think most fat chicks try to hide the body parts they're ashamed of. I'm not really all that different. I hate my upper arms with their weird bat-wing-like flappiness. But sometimes I buy things like this beautiful gown that shows off those arms. It's like my own challenge to myself. If I can make it through a night with my worst parts hanging out, I can make it through anything anyone else throws at me.

That was a lesson I learned in college. Along with blowjobs.

Another bonus of having a date is not having to deal with driving and parking myself. When I finally got down to the event hall the firm had rented, I'd about had it with Saturday-night-party traffic. I opted for the valet parking because it was easier. I exchanged my keys for a little green piece of paper, which I slipped into my blue satin clutch, and sashayed my way into the party. I was a couple minutes late—another thing people expected of me at social events, but never at trial—so the ballroom was already mostly full.

When I was growing up, a swanky night out was dinner at a chain restaurant that served lobster. Even though at this point I'd been to more than my share of these black-tie events because of my job, my breath always caught at the first sight of the room. I sometimes felt like Cinderella at the ball. Tuxedos make all men look good—my firm belief—and every woman is a princess in a ball gown.

Tonight was no different. Muted light from the chandeliers and candle sconces created a fairy-tale feel in the room. Light twinkled off rhinestones and diamonds; the deep melodies of big-band music shifted through the air; a few couples danced to the tune, heels clinking and gowns swishing.

Yep. Cinderella.

I tore my gaze away and concentrated on the faces around the room. Cody, my work-husband, was supposed to be here with his real-life wife, June. And I had to be sure to make nice with the firm partners. I would be up for a spot on the shingle later in the year, so some hand-shaking and smiling was the order of the evening.

I realized that I didn't actually know very many people here. Crenshaw & Rhodes usually did mostly corporate work—mergers, takeovers, contract negotiations— so the company's social gatherings often saw all the same folks. This was the rare pro bono event, which brought a whole different set of people coming out to support the cause: sponsoring the erection of a new building for Helping Hands. It was about time too. The old building was in horrible condition. Pipes leaked into the walls of the sleeping areas. Black mold in the kitchen. Every weekend I volunteered there—which was most weekends when I wasn't working—I ended up cleaning mold and fallen plaster from the disrepair. It wasn't for lack of trying when it came to upkeep. Jessie and Annette, the women who ran it, did their best. The building was just shitty.

So Crenshaw & Rhodes stepped in to spearhead fund-raisers for a replacement. This evening wasn't just a fund-raiser, though. It was also a celebration. Work on the new building was to start this week. And speaking of Annette…

"Caly! God, you look gorgeous! I don't think I've ever seen you dressed up." She fairly tackled me in a huge hug, somehow managing not to spill her glass of bubbly. The scent of roses lingered around me long after she let me go.

"Well, I don't think three-inch pumps are a good fashion choice when it comes to scrubbing floors and serving spaghetti."

Annette guffawed in that way she does, loud and from the belly. "That's true." She was a short woman, but round in all the nicest places. Her prematurely gray hair was piled on the top of her head and speared through with little flower buds. She wore a very colorful knee-length dress that actually looked great on her. I don't know that anyone else could have pulled it off.

Jessie suddenly appeared at her side—she did that sometimes—dressed in a smart gray pantsuit with black ankle boots. Her short brown hair was its usual tousled mess. Not many older women could handle that cut. But it suited Jessie like it was created for her. She held her hand out to me, a very somber expression on her face. "I want to thank you."

*Oh God, here we go again.* "Why?" I shook her hand, because it would have been rude not to. But the thanks were starting to get on my nerves.

"For arranging all this."

"I didn't arrange anything. I'm just an employee. The partners are the ones who saw your need and made all this happen."

"But not without a push from you. They never would have done it on their own."

"She's right," Annette added. "You know that."

*Meh.* The quickest way to get this over with... "Well, you're welcome. Tell me you're going to relax and have a good time." I smiled. I really was overjoyed about this too, even with the excessive thanks.

"Oh yes!" Annette leaned in and dropped her voice. "They have champagne." She lifted the flute in her hand by way of emphasis.

Warmth and love washed over me. Annette was such a kind, free spirit. I felt blessed to have her in my life. "Just don't enjoy it too much. I don't know about you, but champagne always leaves me with a headache in the morning."

Annette pshawed at me, and Jessie gave her the affectionate look she always did.

"We're going to enjoy tonight," Jessie said. "Because the next few months are going to be long."

I'd never been part of planning a building before—not that I was part of it now. I really hadn't been lying when I said that I wasn't very involved in the project. Most of the information I got about the project came from Annette and Jessie.

"Weren't you supposed to meet the building team today?" I asked.

"We did!" Annette's eyes twinkled. "I was hoping we'd be at your office, but we met at the architect's. He was there and the man who will be supervising the actual building. We also met one of the bankers who is involved. We had to sign a bunch of papers."

*Papers?* "I thought you weren't signing anything until they're ready to break ground?"

"They're doing that week after next," Jessie said.

"Wow. That's right around the corner. I had no idea it was coming up that fast." I grinned. "I'm pretty out of the loop."

"We actually told them at the meeting that we would like you to have a bigger part in the whole project."

Well that wasn't what I meant at all. "You did?"

A server came by and offered his tray of champagne flutes to us. Jessie waved him off before Annette could even reach for another glass, but I managed to snag one before he left. The bubbly was sweet and went down easily. I'd have to be careful. It was too enticing. And I hadn't been kidding about the headaches.

"Yes," Annette said. "We want you to be involved. We trust you."

"Thank you. I appreciate your confidence in me. I've never done anything like that before, though."

"Neither have we." Jessie gave me an upturn at the corner of her mouth—she wasn't very gregarious in the most happy of circumstances, so I took that as a win.

Something caught Annette's attention behind me. "Oh! There's Mr. Crenshaw and the architect man. I am horrible with names. What's his name, Jess?"

I turned and saw Brad approaching. Just to his right walked, apparently, the architect.

"I don't remember his last name," Jessie said. "It's on the papers at home, though. His first name is Evan."

"Yes," I said. "Evan Morrell."

# Chapter Two

I admit to not being able to breathe for a moment. Evan Morrell had looked good last night in his suit and loosened tie. But now…

He wasn't even in the same class as all the other men in their monkey suits. He wore a frock-coat-style jacket that fell just below his hips over a dark silver vest. The short lapels were lined in satin, and the three buttons below had been left unfastened. Instead of a bow tie, he wore a long tie, fluffed out, in a silver that matched the vest. That color complemented his skin and deepened the brown of his eyes.

My heartbeat raced. And I hated that it did.

"Annette, Jessie, it's so good to see you." My boss, Brad Crenshaw, kissed each of their hands. Annette giggled. "Caly, you look beautiful. Have you met Evan Morrell? He's the architect designing the new shelter building." Brad made the polite pointings—as if I wouldn't figure out he was introducing the guy next to him. "Evan, this is Caly Arling. I believe she's going to be working more closely on this project from here on out." He flashed his work smile at Annette, who beamed. I offered my hand.

"Ms. Arling, it's a pleasure." It was like a strange echo from last night. Evan Morell took my hand, then raised it to his lips, giving me an amused half grin as he did. He brushed his lips over my knuckles, his gaze locked on mine. A twinkle deepened in his eye.

Heat flushed over my whole body. I couldn't work out whether I wanted to jump him or punch him. And I'm not generally a violent sort of person. I also couldn't tell whether he was trying to keep our previous meeting a secret or not. Either way, two could play that game.

"I look forward to working with you, Mr. Morrell." I slid my fingers from his and took a sip of my champagne. I tried not to gulp it down.

"Yes, it should be a good project, I think. An interesting one." He grinned openly, and Annette giggled again. She caught my eye and winked. I waited for her to break out into cheers. I swear, nothing gets past that woman.

I was also a bit annoyed at how easily she was figuring out the situation. People sometimes mistook Annette's guilelessness for a lack of intelligence. They were always sadly mistaken. She could read people like no one I have ever known.

"So, we break ground a week from Thursday," Brad said, mostly addressing the other women. I turned my attention to him, but remained keenly aware of Evan Morrell at my side. "You ladies will be there, I know. Caly, how about you?"

"I absolutely wouldn't miss it."

"You know," Annette said, her voice bursting with excitement, "Caly has been with us for years. She's probably our longest-running, most consistent volunteer."

Brad's bushy eyebrows went up, and his gaze swung to me. "Really? I had no idea."

"Most weekends, she's with us. She's done so much work around the old building. I'm very excited that she's going to be working on this. She deserves to see the fruits of her labors."

"Annette..." I looked to Jessie and hoped my pleading came through my eyes.

One corner of Jessie's mouth quirked just a bit, and then she became my guardian angel by turning the conversation in a different direction. "Mr. Morrell, thank you so much for contributing your time and resources. I hope you know how grateful we all are. Once everything is finished, we will be hosting a party for all those who helped, as well as for the folks who will be helped by this new building. If you don't mind rubbing elbows with those of us who are a bit lower on the totem pole, we would love for you to attend." Jessie, who is very, very smart, did not give him a chance to respond. "I will be sure to send an invitation to your office. All of your staff are welcome, of course." She tipped her head toward the group, and she winked again. "There won't be champagne, though, sadly."

Everyone was silent for a moment, and Brad looked like he wanted to flee, but then Evan Morrell surprised me and broke out into a great laugh.

"Jessie, it would be my absolute pleasure to rub elbows with you and yours. Please count me as a yes." Then he leveled those brown eyes at me. "Will you be attending, Ms. Arling?"

I had eight different sentences I wanted to start, and none of them led in the same direction. Apparently, I took so long to decide on one, Annette felt the need to come to my rescue.

"Of course she'll be there. There is no way we will let her miss it."

Evan's Morrell's smile widened a touch—his left-side dimple deepened—and amusement played in his eyes again. "Very good."

A tingle slipped through my limbs and gathered in my lower abdomen. *Dammit.* I did not want to be attracted to him. Especially not this attracted, for fuck's sake. This wasn't like when I'm hunting. When I'm hunting, I'm in control. I wasn't in control of those damn tingles.

"Jess," Annette said, holding up her empty flute. "Let's go get some champagne. Just one more." Her smile lit up her face.

Jessie gave a soft sigh but nodded. "Okay. But just one more. We don't need you dancing on the tables."

"But the music is good!"

Everyone laughed. Jessie and Annette made their good-byes and wandered off. Brad looked at his architect. "I'm going to leave you in Caly's capable hands. My wife has been giving me hand signals from across the room since we got over here. If I ignore her much longer, she may not go home with me tonight."

Nods all around, and then I was alone with him.

"Well, this is an interesting turn of events, yes?"

Interesting was the understatement of the year. "I agree. So when you came into Chemistry last night, you'd just left the signing meeting with Annette and Jessie."

"Yes. It was all the formal contracts for the building site, the loan papers, the official working arrangements among all the participants. Nothing out of the ordinary aside from the fact that it's a charity."

"And you designed the building?" I took another sip of my champagne, but it didn't seem quite as sweet. Maybe it was the metallic taste of nerves that had permeated my mouth.

"Nothing fancy, but it will more than meet their needs. It's multilevel with sleeping rooms on the top floors, office, kitchen, dining, and business area on the lower floor." He put a hand on my elbow and began walking. I didn't have much choice but to move with him.

"Business area?" I hadn't heard anything about that. It mostly distracted me from the tingling his touch made on my skin. Mostly.

"The ladies said that one of their long-term goals was to provide education and job-placement assistance, so I designed an area that can be broken into two classrooms if needed and also has enough electricity and data connections for about a dozen or so computers. It can be expanded to fifteen wired connections and, of course, more if we install a wireless router. We'll talk about the pros and cons of that when we get there."

We ended up near the dance floor, where two couples moved to a moderately slow song.

"You know about computers too?"

A waiter approached, and Evan took my glass and placed it on the waiter's tray. "I know a bit about computer networking. It's useful knowledge in my line of work." He barely paused before saying, "I'd like to dance with you, if you are willing."

Willing. It seemed more and more difficult to keep my breathing even. I really didn't get why this guy had this effect on me. Would spending more time in his company help or make it worse?

He held out his hand, and I hesitated a moment before deciding that it would at least be interesting. I like interesting. I put my hand in his.

He led me onto the floor just as the song ended. A new song began, a slower song. His hand on my waist warmed my skin through the satin. He held me close enough that I could feel his breath against me—a faint smell of mint and something sweet—but not so close that we were pressed together. Propriety and all that.

"Brad mentioned to me that you're up for equity partner soon."

"Really?" Obviously, I knew I was up for equity partner; I'd made junior partner a couple years ago, and equity partner was the next rung on the ladder. I was more interested in the fact that Brad had told him about it. When was I a subject of conversation between them? "Was this before or after you brushed me off last night?"

He didn't say anything right away, but the look on his face wasn't the look of surprise and shame that I'd hoped it would be. No, it was that damn amused look, with his one eyebrow not quite cocked but raised just a little and that fucking twinkle in his eye again. He brought his mouth to my ear, and his breath tickled my skin. In the lowest tone possible, he whispered, "After."

A shiver ran straight down my spine. I was half-afraid that my body shook with it. It took a minute for my brain to actually engage, and then I realized that I had no idea what that even meant. Did it mean he'd asked Brad about me? How had he known I worked there? All the questions that popped up in my head clambered around for priority. This seemed to be common in my interactions with him — being tongue-tied, off balance. And worse — off my game. And that annoyed the fuck out of me.

"Stalking me? Is that what's happening, then?"

His low chuckle rumbled through his chest. "Stalk? No. Inquire? Yes. I'm an inquisitive man."

"I think the difference is subtle."

"That is, perhaps, true." He gave a full smile that engaged his entire face. I'd thought his half-dimpled grin had been gorgeous. This stunned me.

He pulled me a bit closer, and we moved in silence over the dance floor. He led; I followed. After a time, he said, "You are a superstar with those ladies, you know. They worship you."

I was glad we were too close to comfortably be looking at each other, because my cheeks blazed red-hot. "I'm just a volunteer. They're the ones who are the superstars. Did you know they've been running that shelter—or a version of it—for over twenty years? I don't know any people as good as Annette and Jessie. My star pales beside theirs." And it was true.

"I think you don't give yourself enough credit. Although I agree that they are quite the pair."

Again with the vagueness. What did that mean? I was glad to hear the end of the song. Mostly. I separated from him and made the polite clapping noises to match everyone else. "Thank you very much for the dance."

"It was my pleasure. I appreciate your attention." His gaze shifted over my shoulder. "I think someone is waiting for you."

I pivoted and saw Cody on the edge of the dance floor in his rented tux with the dark red tie. He waved me over. I looked back to Evan. "Excuse me, please."

"Of course. I'm sure I will see you later." He dipped his head to me in a slight bow. The formality made my nipples harden. Okay, maybe it was just him, in general. But the bow was hot.

I was both relieved and disappointed to make my way over to my work-husband.

"Hey," he said. "Sorry. Was that a conquest?"

"What? No. He's the architect guy." I couldn't tell if I was blushing or not. I said the words way too fast, though. Cody lifted a brow and then shook his head.

"Okay, good. Never mind about that then. We've got someone for you to meet."

*Oh brother.* "Why does everyone keep trying to set me up? I'm perfectly happy being single, you know."

Cody raised both hands in mock-surrender. "It's not me." He led the way through the crowd to the other side of the room, where a number of round tables had been set up. I'd seen them earlier but hadn't gone over. "It's June. She's the one who seems to want to marry you off." June was Cody's real wife. The nonwork one. Nonwork in all the ways. It wasn't surprising that she occupied her time with playing matchmaker. I couldn't imagine what else she might do with her time. Truth be told, I couldn't actually imagine that much free time.

And there she was. We had broken out of the throngs around the dance floor and June sat at a table with a man in—of course—a tux whose back was to us. She looked beautiful in a pearl gown. It contrasted with her tan skin.

"Oh good. You're here!" She jumped from the chair and held a hand out to me as if we were going to go for a walk through the park. He fingers were cool to the touch. "Come meet Daniel. He works down at the university."

Daniel stood and turned round. He and I met gazes and both burst out laughing. June's look of startled confusion was classic. Cody gave a soft snort behind me.

"June," I said, "Daniel's my cousin." Second cousin, to be exact. We'd grown up playing kickball in my backyard. We'd even been roommates in college before I met Tessa.

June's face turned an alarming shade of red, and she let go of my hand as she sputtered apologies for a moment, her gaze alternating from me to Daniel.

"Don't worry about it," he said and patted June on the arm. "Although I am a bit disappointed since you talked Caly up so much. I was really looking forward to meeting the girl you described. Figures that we'd be related." He laughed and poked me in the arm. "Go find some other awesome guy."

I grinned at him, then turned my attention to June. "I'm sorry. I probably could have shared that information a bit more considerately."

June took a couple gulps of air before she shook her head. "No. It's fine. I just… I don't know. I guess that was the last thing I was expecting."

Cody stepped past me, to June's side and put a hand on her elbow. "Now there you go. Maybe taking a break from matchmaking might be a good idea? Let's get a drink. I think we could both use one." He directed her away, tipping a wink to me as they went.

"Well, that was interesting," I said.

"Hey, want me to set you up with a guy?" Daniel's wide grin made me laugh.

"Let me add you to the list of people trying to get me married off."

"Yeah, I don't care if you become an old spinster in a rocking chair ogling the lawn boy."

I laughed again. "I didn't know you were going to be here."

"The university is donating some older computers from the lab to get them started with their education area or whatever they're doing. So a few of us are doing the rounds and making nice with all the folks involved." Daniel tilted his head toward a group of people near the bar. Brad Crenshaw was among them. "Politics, you know."

"Yeah." I tried to find Evan's dark hair in the group across the room but couldn't.

Our conversation devolved into small talk about the family until we both decided we were bored. With a family-style smooch and a promise to do lunch in the next couple weeks, we split in opposite directions. I checked my watch and realized I'd barely been here an hour. I was ready to go.

I hunted around for a while until I found Annette and Jessie. I said my good-byes with hugs all around and then skipped out. I presented my ticket to the valet and scooted home to change into some more relaxed clothes. Chemistry seemed like a good way to end the evening.

-–⇒⇒⇐⇐–-

It was almost ten by the time I got there. I couldn't decide whether I wanted to hunt or not. I still felt really off my game. Damn Evan Morrell. I'd brought my tablet with me, tucked safely away in my purse, in the event I decided not to hunt after all. At least I could get some work done on the book. Yay for cloud storage.

I settled for a place at the bar, and Kyle, the barkeep tonight, hooked me up with a lemon drop. Out of all the bartenders at Chemistry, he definitely made the best martinis. We had some small talk, and then he went off to tend other customers. I sipped on my martini as I looked down the bar. A couple interesting prospects. A younger guy who looked Hispanic, in a polo and nice-fitting jeans, played darts near the other end.

Guys in their early twenties are always fun, because they've got lots of stamina and they tend to forget to call the next day. I usually hook up with older guys, just because they feel better to me as far as life-experience stuff, but the younger ones definitely had their good points. I made a mental note to include a section on age in the book.

I watched him for a few minutes before he actually realized he was being scoped out. We exchanged smiles, and then it was his turn to throw again. I picked up my glass, swiveled my stool, and slid off it. I still hadn't decided for sure that I wanted to take someone home, but it never hurt to farm the prospects. I scanned the room as I moved down the bar. It also never hurt to keep one's options open.

And… Of course. *There he is.*

In the fourth booth along the wall sat Evan Morrell, now trademark glass of whiskey—or bourbon, or whatever it was—settled on the table in front of him. He looked pretty amazing in a gray polo shirt and what looked like black slacks. I could barely see them under the table. And he gazed directly at me, lifted his glass, and toasted in my direction.

Was he following me? Inquiry or stalking…a subtle difference. It made me want to slap him. It occurred to me that for being mostly a pacifist, I seemed to have an awful lot of feelings of violence toward him.

The dart boy no longer on my agenda, I changed course and went to the side of Evan's table. "What are you doing here?"

He leaned back and waved a hand, indicating the room. "Someone I know told me this is a neighborhood bar. I'm in the neighborhood."

Suddenly, I was teetering on the edge of serious anger, but I'd be damned if I could figure out why the hell I was mad. "I figured you'd have still been at the benefit."

"I could say the same about you." He sipped his drink and then motioned the bench across from him. "Would you like to join me?"

As what was becoming the usual, I could not decide whether I wanted to remain in his company or walk away. And, again as usual, I chose to join him. I set my martini down and eased into the booth. "Thanks."

"Did you enjoy yourself this evening?"

"Yes. It was fine."

"That sounds like tolerated. Not enjoyed."

I lifted a shoulder. "It's not my scene."

"No," he said. "It's not."

What the hell did that mean? "Why do you always do that?"

"What?" He didn't look concerned at my anger.

"You make statements like you know me."

"I do. We met yesterday. We danced this evening. Now we are sharing a table and a drink together." His dark eyes seemed to glitter in the reflected light from the rest of the room. He had a perfect smile too. Damn him for being hot.

"That's not what I mean, and I think you know it."

He swirled the amber liquid at the bottom of his glass. "I know it, do I?" He peered at me. "You don't think you're giving me more credit than I deserve?"

That sounded like a trick question, but I couldn't work out what the trick was. So I just didn't answer. He watched me with what looked like an indulgent half grin. Anger thrummed in me. So fucking condescending.

Finally, he said, "Why did you approach me last night?"

I lifted my glass and took a long sip—a really long sip, actually. "I didn't recognize you, and I thought you might want a welcome."

"The welcome-wagon thing again, eh?"

"What's wrong with that?" Everything felt hot—my skin, my muscles. I was wound tight, as if one prick would pop me like an overinflated balloon.

"Nothing at all." He swirled his glass again. "If it were true. But you didn't approach me because I seemed like I needed a friendly face."

I just sat there, sort of disconnected. Inside, I struggled to follow what he was talking about. Anger and confusion and attraction and belligerence warred inside me for a place on top. *Get it together, Caly! Jesus.* I finally found my tongue. "No? So why did I approach you, since you seem to have all the answers?"

He straightened from the relaxed, leaned-back posture he'd been in and sat squarely on the seat, his elbows on the table and hands flat. "You play games in here. You approached me because you wanted to play your game." He paused and stared at me for a moment before resuming. "But you and I...we don't play the same game. And that is why you are unsteady, because the rules of my game are different."

Everything in me fluttered from my heart right on down. But God, he was being so arrogant. "What the hell are you talking about?" When all else fails, act like you don't know what the fuck is going on.

He leaned back again and draped one arm along the top of his bench seat. The intensity of his brown-eyed gaze bored into me. My skin tingled.

The silence lengthened from tolerable to good-God-this-is-awkward.

"So we're done? You're not even going to answer me?" Anger itched in the back of my mind again. He *was* playing games. And regardless of whose rules they were, I didn't like it. Not at all.

Evan lifted his glass, took the final mouthful of his liquor, and said, with a casual air, "I wonder if there's anything behind all those masks you wear. If someone were to pull them all away—the professional, the volunteer, the huntress"—he put emphasis on this last word—"I wonder what he would find."

I found myself dumbstruck—because apparently that was going to be my role with him always—while he pulled out his wallet. He deposited a twenty on the table and slid out of the seat.

"Good evening, Ms. Arling. I will see you Monday."

I may have stammered something, but he was already gone by the time I actually found my brain again.

*Dammit.*

# Chapter Three

I spent the night alternately fuming and pondering. I couldn't figure out why this guy affected me so much. Evan kept me off my footing; he said things that left me tongue-tied; and a look from him set my skin tingling—and, if I thought about it, left my pussy damp. Okay, more than damp.

Sleep took a while, and two orgasms, before it found me. When it did, it brought strange dreams about a dark man standing so close behind me I could feel his breath on my nape. He whispered to me, but the words came through garbled, muffled. But despite that, his voice seemed to make me hot and then hotter. I ground back against him, and he moved his hands to my hips. He held me in place and let me move against him but did nothing himself but continue his soft, insistent whispers.

I woke up with my hand between my thighs, an old '80s Brit-pop song blaring on my alarm, and Evan Morrell on my mind. *Guh.*

---

It was almost evening—I'd spent the day working on a case for later in the week—before I remembered that I'd committed to dinner with Tessa, Gordon, and whoever today's man du jour was. I really was not in the mood. Normally, I was at least game to see if someone was tumble-able. I mean, I should be able to get a lay out of these matchmaking attempts, right?

But I wasn't even in the mood for that. It all just seemed tiring and tedious. And added to that, the whole conversation from Chemistry last night kept playing on a continual loop in my head. Now that I was further away from the experience, I turned it over and started analyzing.

Evan Morrell got under my skin, obviously. Something about him—his eyes, his scent, whatever—made me into a dumb girl. And when I hit that mental space, my brain seemed to just stop functioning. That was the most frustrating part. He definitely spoke in riddles and vagueness, but I'm way smarter than I act when I'm around him. Even now, I still wasn't sure what he had been getting at about the masks. I mean, yes, I put a certain face out depending on where I am, who I'm with. But everyone does that. I didn't understand what made him zero in on that with me.

My phone buzzed on the table beside me.

*Tessa: You're still coming tonight, right?*

*Me: Can I beg off?*

*Tessa: No.*

*Me: Meh. Then I guess I'm still coming.*

*Tessa: Great! :) Wear something pretty.*

Well, then I guess it was settled.

-→➤➤◄◄◄--

Something pretty turned out to be linen slacks and a button-down, gauzy blouse in dark blue. I really didn't feel like putting any more effort into it. I did my makeup and put some gel in my short hair, tossed on a pair of earrings and done was done.

I was late, apparently, because there was an unfamiliar vehicle—an Audi—in their driveway when I arrived at Tessa's split-level townhouse. An unexpected thought flashed through my head. What if the man du jour was Evan? My heart raced, and I had a really weird mix of fear and excitement.

My emotional split personality was starting to annoy me.

I knocked on the door and then let myself in. "Looks like everyone's already here," I said loudly, as I closed the door behind me. They were gathered in the small living room to the left of the front door. I handed Tessa the bottle of merlot I'd brought and stood still for her to hug me.

"I'm so glad you're here!" She turned to the men and motioned to the new guy, who I admit was pretty good-looking. "This is Thomas Ramiro. Thomas, my best friend, Caly Arling."

The awkward shaking of hands and pleasant words ensued as Tessa went off in search of the bottle opener. Gordon, always a man of few words, stood quietly as Thomas and I navigated the being-set-up waters.

Tessa obviously knew my taste in men. Thomas was tall and well-built, though not overly built. Dark, wavy hair topped a friendly face with hazel eyes and full lips. His skin, a caramel color, reminded me for a split second of Evan, and then I pushed the thought firmly away. I was not going to get caught up on *that* particular merry-go-round again. When Thomas spoke, I detected a faint accent—Spanish, probably.

"Tessa tells me you're an attorney?"

"Yes. Corporate, mainly, though I occasionally do pro bono work."

"For all the jokes about how terrible lawyers are, every one I've known has been a good person."

"Well... Thank you for that." This was an odd conversation already. "I try to live well and help others. What do you do?"

"I'm a therapist."

*Great. Hey, Doc, I can't get this other guy who makes me crazy out of my head. What should I do?*

"I work in drug rehab and with other addiction programs."

"You must have very interesting days."

He grinned, and it was nice. Friendly and open. "Sometimes, yes."

Tessa returned carrying a small tray with four wineglasses, already full. "Here we go." Once everyone had their glass, including the silent Gordon, she raised hers. "To new friendships."

This was starting to seem like a cheesy movie, but I lifted my glass, clinked, and took a great mouthful. I pick good wine, if I do say so myself.

The evening actually got a bit better. Thomas turned out to be a very laid-back, fun guy with a good sense of humor. We made eye contact a lot, and I felt a little bit of chemistry working between us that seemed promising. Dinner was Gordon's amazing homemade pasta with meatballs along with a salad and then fruit compote for dessert. By the end of the evening, I had a very light buzz and was glad I hadn't bailed. Thomas was a nice guy, and I realized I'd missed Tessa a lot. I resolved to make sure we could do lunch soon.

Just after ten, Thomas stood and said, "Well, Monday morning comes early. I should probably head out. Tessa, thank you for the invitation and, Gordon, I want to get your sauce recipe from you. That was incredible!"

"I need to get going too." I rose and gathered up my purse. "I've got a meeting in the morning for the shelter build." With Evan, among others.

"Oh, you're a part of that?" Thomas asked, his attention now firmly on me. He looked delighted.

"Yes. I'm with Crenshaw & Rhodes." It seemed like everyone I met these days was involved with the shelter build in some way.

"That's really wonderful. Jessie and Annette are amazing people, and I am so glad your firm took an interest in them."

"You know them?" How small the world was surprised me sometimes.

"Yes. I've worked with a number of their guests over the years. They often refer me those people who are struggling with their addictions."

I wondered how I'd never heard of Thomas before. Why hadn't Annette tried to set us up? *Okay, Caly, now you're losing it. Wanting people to set you up.*

"I'll walk you out," Thomas said.

"All right." I gave him what I hoped was a winning smile, then said my good-byes and love-yous to Tessa and Gordon. Tessa gave me an extra squeeze and a grin. I rolled my eyes at her. She just laughed.

Thomas and I stepped out onto the porch, and he waited while I descended the few stairs to the postage-stamp yard. We walked together along the short path to the driveway.

"Would I be too forward if I asked to see you again?" he said as we reached my car.

This sounded less like a hookup and more like a let's-date line of conversation. I thought about whether I wanted to date someone for serious. I was used to the hookups, and the idea of dating made me a little uncomfortable, but I couldn't tell if it was dating itself or because I *was* so used to hooking up instead. That would require a lot more thought. "No," I said. "Not forward at all."

"Good. Because I would absolutely like to see you again. I don't want to keep you tonight, though, so I'll get your number from Tessa?"

"Sure." I'd unlocked the door with my key fob and now stood facing him with my back to the car. The interaction didn't seem over yet. If I were taking him home, I'd know exactly what to do. As it was, I felt a bit lost. I was not liking this whole forgot-how-to-deal-with-men vibe I'd been having lately.

"I enjoyed dinner tonight." Thomas leaned closer, but only a little. I had plenty of time to shift back or step away if I wanted to. I stayed put. "May I kiss you?"

I didn't think a man could surprise me anymore. But no one had ever asked for permission to kiss me. Granted, normally I was the one who instigated smooches. Instead of answering, I relied on my experience and tiptoed up—he was taller than I realized—and pressed my lips to his. His mouth was soft, the skin silky. He leaned down into me and put his palm against the side of my face. The kiss remained chaste, and I didn't part my lips. I analyzed everything about the kiss, from the feel and the texture of his lips to the taste of him—a bit of wine with a background of tartness.

He drew back, and when I opened my eyes, he was smiling down on me. "Thank you," he said softly.

I adjusted the strap of my purse on my shoulder—*hello, awkward, it's been a minute*—and tilted back until I was leaning against the car. "I'll talk to you later, then?"

"Yes, most certainly."

"Have a good night." I popped the door open and dropped into the seat.

"You too. Sweet dreams." He pushed my door closed and then walked around the front of my car as I started the engine.

-->>-<<-

I wasn't even out of the subdivision when my phone rang. I took it on my headset. Of course, it was Tessa.

"So?"

"So what?"

"How was it?"

"How was what?" I knew what she wanted. I was just still off my game enough to not want to give it to her, mainly because I wasn't really sure what was going on with *me*.

"Thomas, you goof. How was it with Thomas?" She sounded breathless over the phone.

"It was fine. He seems like a nice enough guy."

"Oh." All the emotion behind a rejection in that one syllable. "So nothing?"

"I didn't say nothing. We exchanged a smooch at the car. He's going to ask you for my number."

"And I can give it to him?" Renewed hope.

"Yes, you can give it to him."

"Yay!"

I laughed. I had to. If you knew Tessa on paper, you'd think she was a pretentious bitch, what with having grown up in Manhattan and attended European boarding school all during high school. But you'd be totally wrong. And changing her major from business to early childhood ed in college was the smartest thing she could have done. Tessa was born to be a teacher. And her temperament matched.

"So," she said, "you're going to go out with him."

"We'll probably get a meal or something. See if we can hold up a conversation without your help."

She sputtered, and I laughed again.

"Not fair, Caly."

"Yeah. Yeah."

"Oh! He just texted me for your number."

"Good timing. I'm about to pull into my lot." Not that her getting a text had anything to do with my apartment's parking lot.

"You'll tell me all about it?"

"My parking lot?"

"Caly."

"Yes, of course. Now let me go so I don't take out a lamppost."

"Oh, all right. I'll talk to you later."

"Yup."

I put the car in Park and sat there looking at the steering wheel.

Thomas was nice enough. But I wished I could stop thinking about Evan.

# Chapter Four

Monday brought three depositions before lunch. It was a rough morning. I was late to the eleven o'clock shelter meeting because my client from the ten o'clock depo wouldn't leave. He just kept talking and talking and talking. I finally had to dump him on my paralegal. Sometimes clients were more clingy than lovers.

"Ms. Arling." Brad always called us by our last names in the office. It was his nod to the formality of the legal tradition. At least, that's what he said.

"Mr. Crenshaw." I took a seat at the conference table and pulled out my tablet and Bluetooth keyboard. Evan gave me a half smile of greeting that didn't quite engage his dimple. I wasn't surprised to see him. The meeting was about Helping Hands, of course. And after his parting shot when he'd said he'd see me Monday, I couldn't have been less surprised. There were two other men there whom Brad introduced as the general contractor—sort of a project manager, apparently—and an electrical engineer.

"We're going over the finalized blueprints, particularly the wiring, and the contractor's lists." Brad motioned to the papers laid out across the surface. I couldn't tell whether he didn't think I would know what a blueprint was, or if he just thought I was dumb in general. "I've included you in this meeting because the ladies requested that you have more involvement."

"Thank you," I said with as level a voice as possible. It was clear from his tone that he wasn't actually interested in having me there. Not that I blamed him, since I had no background in this sort of thing. But it still grated on me. Evan watched me, but I didn't make eye contact. I already felt on the verge of that scattered feeling I always got when I interacted with him. I didn't need it here at work.

Brad carried on with what presumably had been happening prior to my late arrival. I tried not to space out during the discussions, but this really wasn't my forte at all. And worse, it was boring. I can get into just about anything if it doesn't make me want to go to sleep. This really made me want to go to sleep.

I pulled up my deposition notes on my tablet and started annotating them, still listening with half an ear about suppliers and delivery schedules. This distraction kept me from being tempted to look at Evan, who was likely not paying me any mind now, since he was actively involved in the conversation around me.

At 11:49, Brad announced he had a lunch meeting to attend and ended our little version of Purgatory. I decided I was going to tell Annette and Jessie that I was just fine being out of the loop. I couldn't imagine a bigger waste of my time. I had real work to do. At least I'd gotten through a part of the deposition notes. I stood and began gathering up my things when Evan appeared at my side.

"Do you have lunch plans?"

My tummy did a little flip-flop, and at the same time, a low feeling of dread cycled through my body. Having lunch together would require me to look at him, I was pretty sure. I couldn't decide whether I was relieved not to have plans or annoyed because I didn't. Apparently a bit of both.

"No. I don't think so." I slid my tablet into my purse.

"I'm going to the Italian place around the corner if you would care to join me."

I still hadn't looked at him. Maybe I *could* get through lunch without eye contact. Because, I realized, I did want to go to lunch with him. Arrogance and all. "Okay. But you'll have to wait a few minutes."

"That's fine. I'll meet you downstairs."

I didn't really need to do anything. I could have left immediately. What I did need was time to gather myself. After he left the conference room, I went back to my office, closed the door, and sat there. I took deep breaths and envisioned myself at lunch with him acting like normal Caly, not weird Caly. I did normal office things, like shut down my computer, straighten my desk, check my phone.

I had a missed call and a voice mail. I didn't recognize the number.

"Hi, Caly. This is Thomas. I just wanted to say again what a good time I had last night. I'd love to see you again. Give me a call so we can compare schedules." He left his number, which matched the caller ID. I saved it to my contacts and then tossed the phone into my purse.

Good. Normal.

Evan waited for me in the lobby of the office building. He sat on a leather bench near the wall, checking his phone. He looked edible in his charcoal-gray business suit with the pale blue shirt and red tie. It occurred to me that he would probably look weird to me in jeans at this point. I'd seen him in business suits and formal wear. Seeing him casual would be very odd.

I resolved to be cool.

"Hey. Sorry for the delay," I said when I'd approached.

He looked up, and his dark eyes undid me. My heart pattered faster, and I struggled to keep my breathing even. "No problem. Have phone, will work." He smiled that full smile, which lit his face, and then slid his phone into his inner jacket pocket. "Ready?"

Where was the aloof, arrogant guy from last night? He seemed almost...friendly. It was weird. Maybe this was just another tactic to put me off my game.

"Yep."

We walked the block and a half to Salvatore's, the small Italian eatery with possibly the best gnocchi I've ever had. There was more than one reason to have accepted this invitation. We talked about the meeting; I admitted I really had no idea what had been going on. He explained a few things until, apparently, my eyes glazed over. Luckily, by then, we'd arrived.

"Miss Caly! Very good to see you again." Veronica, the seventeen-year-old daughter of the owner, greeted me with a hug. I'd known her since she was eleven and ran around, spaghetti sauce always somewhere on her, getting under her mom's feet. Now she looked like an adult and much more sophisticated in her sleeveless sundress at the hostess stand. It suddenly made me feel old. "On the patio?"

I looked to Evan to see if that was okay. He had a grin on his face and looked almost impish, like he was immensely pleased with something. I had no idea what that could be. He nodded, and Veronica led the way. We settled into a bistro table near the water fountain sculpture, and she left us with a couple menus. A few of the surrounding tables had patrons, but the full lunch crowd hadn't arrived yet.

"You're well loved," Evan said as he opened a menu. I studied him, trying to decide whether he was being facetious or not. He didn't seem to be.

"I've been coming here for years. I've known the family for a long time."

He spent a few moments reading, and then, without raising his gaze, he said, "You're not going to look at the menu?"

"I already know what I am getting."

Then he looked at me. That intensity behind his eyes was just like last night. "And what are you getting?"

I stammered for a second, to which he smiled. And then, just like that, I was annoyed at him again. Almost angry. "The gnocchi."

"Is it your favorite?"

I didn't want to give him that information. I didn't want to give him *any* information. *Argh! Why is this so crazy? Why am I acting like an idiot?* "Yes."

"Ah, good."

When our server—Georges, who also hugged me— arrived with two glasses of water, I ordered the gnocchi and then so did Evan. I knew I must have had the universe's dumbest surprised look on my face. He laughed. I didn't think he'd ever actually laughed in front of me before. Smirks, yes. Amused grins, yes. Never a laugh. Georges left, and Evan said, "You are not the only person in the world who likes gnocchi, you know."

*Well, duh.* "I just didn't figure you for one of them."

"Really? I love gnocchi. It's not easy to do well. And I've observed that you have pretty good taste, so I think it's worth the risk."

"Good taste, huh? I'm not sure you've ever observed my taste."

He held up a hand and counted off on his fingers. "Lemon-drop martini. Not my favorite, but if one is going to drink a fruity drink, then it is much better than a strawberry daiquiri or some other such." Second finger. "The young man playing darts. Again, not my favorite, but not a bad-looking choice." Third finger. "Helping Hand. You've volunteered there for years without taking credit in any way. And that counts as two." Fourth finger.

Heat flushed my cheeks. He paid a bit more attention than I realized. I didn't know what to say, so I said what always worked in situations like these. "Thank you."

He gave a little nod. "You're welcome."

I took a sip of my water, unrolled my silverware, spread my napkin on my lap, smoothed it out twice, and took another sip of water. I didn't look at him.

"Are you ready?"

I jerked my gaze up to him. "What?"

"Are you ready?"

"Ready for what?" I felt like a parrot.

"To ask some of the questions that are rambling around in that brain of yours."

Here I was, tense, nervous, flustered. And he sat there, leaned back, jacket unbuttoned, tie unfastened just a little bit, looking relaxed, like he was about to leave for a vacation. I took a deep breath and tried to channel some of his calm.

"All right. Questions," I said. "What did you mean last night about games?"

"Which part?"

"You said you play a different game. What does that mean? And no vague answers." I didn't want him evading the question.

"I watched you last evening, the evening before. You study the crowd, pick your prey, and you zero in for the kill. The kill, in this case, is likely you taking him home to bed. I haven't seen you close a deal, but because of your hunting style, I don't think you look for anything beyond the one night." He gave that half smile. "Is that not-vague enough so far?"

I only nodded. I didn't really trust my voice right now. He obviously had me pegged. Although I had no idea how.

"While my game is similar, in a way, I don't play for one night." He paused, which stood to underscore his words. "And my rules are vastly different. It isn't just about my bed. It isn't just about a woman's body."

My mind was blank for a moment. *Is he hitting on me?* If so, this was not like pursuit that I was used to.

Saved by the gnocchi. Georges arrived with our bowls and placed one before each of us. After we assured him we didn't need anything—I would be lucky to remember how to work a fork, at this point—he left us to our meals. And I was glad, because this gave us something to concentrate on besides whatever message Evan was trying to send me…which was good, because I had no idea what that was.

"I was right to trust your taste. This is delicious," he said before putting another forkful into his mouth.

"You're welcome." Some corner of my mind registered that the vodka sauce was especially good, but most of my mind was working on turning over his words. I still couldn't figure out whether this was a seduction technique or whether he was just being his arrogant self. Although his tone hadn't come across as arrogant. Just matter-of-fact. "So what is your game?" I finally asked.

He didn't answer right away. He'd just put some pasta into his mouth. But by the glint in his eyes, I suspected that even if he hadn't just taken a bite, he still wouldn't have answered right away. *Bastard.*

"At its base, it is the same game you play. I look at the field, select the most appealing subject, and then zero in for the kill." The upturn of his lips were subtle enough that I wasn't sure I'd seen it. But some things clattered together in my head.

"Is that what you're doing now? Zeroing in for the kill?"

"Do you feel like prey?" His left eyebrow tilted up, and I was sure that I saw another twinkle in his dark eyes.

And then the rest clicked into place. That was why I'd been so off my game. That was why I'd become tongue-tied around him. *Fucker.* He was hunting me—had been this whole time!

I folded my napkin and set it gently on the table beside my mostly eaten lunch. "I think we're done here," I said in my most level, most I-don't-give-a-shit-about-you voice. Gathering my purse as I stood, I glanced at him as rose with me.

"Are you sure?"

"Yes."

"Very well. Thank you for joining me for lunch. I am sure I will see you soon."

I had nothing more to say. I turned on my heel and walked out.

# Chapter Five

I spent the next few days in a perpetual state of pissed-offed-ness. I snapped at my paralegal and was short with the receptionist. It took all my willpower not to bite Cody's head off when he mentioned Evan. Wisely, he didn't ask for any details. I ignored my phone and avoided all the senior partners.

There was only one meeting about Helping Hands, which I didn't attend because of court. Thank God. It was late Friday afternoon before I saw Evan again, and I was surprised to see him walk into Helping Hands dressed in jeans and a T-shirt.

And, as predicted, he looked weird dressed all casually. But it didn't get in the way of his hotness. Oh no. He was still absolutely gorgeous. Of course, Annette and Jessie went gaga over him. I decided that the kitchen was where I was most needed right then.

I jumped into helping the other volunteers, some of them shelter residents, set up dinner. We'd just finished getting the veggies chopped and into the stockpot for the stew when Jessie came in looking for me. "You disappeared."

"Well, no. Mostly I walked into the kitchen."

She narrowed her eyes at me—that shrewd look that meant she probably got the whole scenario. "Not in a friendly mood?"

"Not particularly, no."

"Mmm. He's volunteered to help with dinner tonight."

I stopped stirring the stew. "Are you kidding me?"

"Nope. Not kidding."

"Fuck."

"Very not friendly."

"No, very not. Keep him on the line? I'll stay in the dining room."

Jessie peeked over the edge of the pot and looked at the stew, which prompted me to stir again. "If that's what you want to do," she said.

"It'd be for the best, I think. Is he planning to stay through cleanup?"

"I believe so."

"Fuck."

"Do you need to leave before then?" Jessie had a way of being sincere in her offering while at the same time challenging you to turn her down.

I pulled the spoon out of the stew and covered the pot. I adjusted the flame to medium-low and gave a big sigh. "No, I'm not going to leave. You know me better than that."

Jessie gave me her patented I-knew-you-could-do-it smile, which was actually surprisingly thin and disdainful-looking. "I do know you better than that. But let me know if you need me, yes?"

"Yes."

After she left, I tried to be pleasant to the folks I shared the kitchen with, all the while trying to work out how I could avoid interacting with Evan all night. As it turned out, I couldn't, because he'd decided he was going to interact with me.

Before we even opened the doors for the residents and others who would be fed, Evan approached me. "I didn't see you at the meeting yesterday."

"I was in court." This game of cat and mouse was grating on my nerves. "Why are you here?"

"I'm volunteering."

"You've never volunteered here before. Why now?" For the first time, I wasn't tongue-tied or flustered. I wasn't blushing, and I wasn't stammering. I was just tired of the game altogether.

"Why do you think?"

I stared at him. He didn't get to ask me questions. When something like a minute had gone by and he hadn't given me a proper reply, I said, "I'm not dealing with your bullshit. If you're not going to be straightforward or honest, then I'm walking away."

"The last time I was straightforward and honest you did walk away."

Okay. That was true. But I wasn't going to give him the benefit of telling him that. I just stood and waited.

"You know why I'm here. Because I wanted to speak to you."

"You own a telephone."

"I do, yes." Apparently, he wasn't biting.

I sighed. "I'm tired of your game, Evan. Okay, your rules are different. Big deal. It's tiring. Exhausting, even."

He watched me for a moment, the corners of his mouth turned up just a little. I couldn't read his expression. It wasn't a smirk, and it wasn't amusement. Well, not snarky amusement, anyway. Maybe just regular amusement. He spread his hands in an open gesture. "This isn't my game. This part is your game. My game comes later, perhaps."

"This is part of the problem. You talk in riddles. Nothing you say is clear." A woman with two small children approached the stew station that Evan was supposed to be manning. I nodded in that direction. "The doors are open. You should get to work."

---

I spent the whole dinner hour—which was really just over two hours—out in the dining room, cleaning up, talking to people and, again, avoiding Evan. Several times when I looked at the serving line, he met my gaze, but I looked away immediately. He said this part was my game, but this was not the way I played. I didn't hook anyone and then play them along. I either went for it, or I didn't. No vagueness.

Had he hooked me? That was part of what had pissed me off at lunch earlier in the week. It had taken a while for me to realize I *was* interested in him. He wasn't my normal type. I had to admit to myself that he absolutely wasn't prey. But I didn't want to be prey either. And it was infuriating that he saw me that way.

I was scrubbing down a table when Annette came over, broom in hand. Usually Annette oversaw the dining-room cleanup while Jessie helped out with the kitchen. Even after all these years, I had no idea how they did the office work or any of the other hassles that come with running anything, because they were always out with the residents, or rather, the guests—which is what they insisted all the volunteers call those who came for a meal.

"So he's a hard worker," she said as she swept under the table I'd just finished wiping down.

"Who?" As if I didn't know.

"Mr. Morrell."

"I'm sure you can call him Evan, Annette."

"I like calling him Mr. Morrell." She grinned at me, little hairs that escaped her bun wisping around her head. "It makes the whole thing seem so important."

I straightened from over the table next to her. "It *is* important. It always has been. Him coming and volunteering doesn't make it more important than before he came."

"Oh, I know, dear. But you bristle so much whenever he's around, so it's also very amusing to watch your reaction when I give him all the extra respect." She winked and gave my upper arm a little pinch.

*Grrr*. So now it was a big joke. I leaned down and began scrubbing the table hard.

"Oh, don't be like that. I'm only teasing." She put her hand over my scrubbing one, causing me to still. I looked up at her, and her gentle expression eased my chaos a little bit. "There's something between you two. We saw it from that first time at the benefit. I think you should see where it goes."

"See where what goes? I mean, he hasn't hit on me. He hasn't asked me out"—except to lunch…and to join him for a drink, both of which ended annoyingly for me—"or done any of the normal 'I like you' things."

"Not everyone speaks the same language when it comes to courting."

*Courting*. What an archaic word. Was that what was happening? Is courting supposed to be confusing? The word itself scared me. Too much commitment.

"So for some reason, you think he's interested in me?"

Annette leaned back a bit and looked at me, wide-eyed. "Of course. It's completely obvious."

"I think you and I have different ideas of what 'completely obvious' means."

Her light, tinkling laugh rang out, and although I didn't really feel it, I smiled in return. "It's all right, dear. But I do hope that you at least consider it."

I wiped down a corner, gave Annette a small kiss on the cheek, and moved on to the last table.

Did Annette even know what she was talking about? She often came across as an earth mother, hippie sort, but she had a really sharp mind that she didn't share with people very often. Jessie was shrewd in an obvious way. Annette was shrewd in the sort of way that jumped out from behind a bush and startled you. Like a ninja.

I didn't know whether I wanted to start anything with Evan. I was pretty happy with my one-night stands. Did I want something else? And this was all supposing Annette wasn't imagining things. And even if she *wasn't*, what exactly did Evan want from me? And why was I even thinking this way?

-→➤➤◄◄◄-

After cleanup, most of the volunteers headed home. The residents scattered to the common room or the sleeping areas. A few went outside to smoke or socialize. I joined them and sat on a low wall that bordered the edge of the tiny backyard that was mostly vegetable garden. Or would be soon. The sun had just set, and shadows had evened out into darkness. I sipped on some iced tea. Annette made the best, sweetest iced tea ever.

I'd thought Evan had left but apparently not. I recognized his silhouette in the doorway as he paused, probably looking for me in the gloom. Just seeing him made my heartbeat speed up. I tried not to wonder what it meant that I recognized him by his body. He spoke to someone smoking on the patio, and she pointed in my direction. *Dammit.* And there he came.

"I didn't want to leave without saying good-bye," he said, looking up at me.

"So Annette seems to think you're interested in dating me or something. She wasn't very clear on what, exactly." I'm a bulls-by-the-horn sort of girl, most of the time, when I wasn't completely flustered by some architect I'd met.

"Does she?" It was too dark to make out any sort of expression on his face. His tone wasn't mocking, though, so maybe Annette wasn't too far off base.

"I just said she does, didn't I?"

He laughed and leaned a shoulder against the wall a few inches from my leg. "Yes. Yes, you did."

"And?"

"And you want to know if she's right?"

I looked down at him. "Are you being dumb intentionally?" Okay, obviously flustered-Caly wasn't around tonight. Thank God. I was getting sick of that bitch.

"She is right in that there is something about you that draws me. Just as I think there's something about me that draws you."

"That's what you think."

"I just said it was, didn't I?" A teasing tone to his voice, and I knew that if the light had been better, I'd have seen that twinkle in his eye. That twinkle that had annoyed me previously but now seemed to give me tingles all of a sudden.

"Touché," I said.

"I think we would play the game well together."

"Your game." I still had no idea what that meant, really. What would it take to get him to be clear, I wondered.

"Yes. My game. It's much more fun than yours."

"Mine is pretty fun."

"For the hunter. Sometimes not as much fun for the prey."

That word again. Heat rose under my skin. "Why do you see me as prey?" Although it was easier interacting with him in the dark, at that moment, I almost wished I could see his face.

"Everyone is hunter to someone." His words were simple and carried no judgment or arrogance in the tone. It sounded more as if he found it to be a positive thing, a benefit. "Everyone is prey to someone. You inspire the hunter in me."

I wasn't sure how to respond to that. So I sat quietly and sipped my tea.

"What did she say about you?"

"What do you mean?"

"Annette seems to think I'm interested in you. What does she think about you?" And this was where he was going to back me into a corner. I probably should have seen it coming. Three miles away.

"She thinks the same of me."

"And is she right?"

Was she? I still wasn't sure. Maybe that was the answer in itself. "I don't know."

"That seems strange for you. Not knowing."

"Yes."

We stayed there, in the silent dark, for another fifteen minutes. A warm breeze blew, tickling the back of my neck. It felt as though something big were happening in the midst of nothing, there in the dark. Finally, he pushed himself off the wall and faced me.

"I am going home. I would like for you to come along, if you are interested in continuing the conversation."

Heat suffused my whole body. Something about his tone perked my nipples and I got goose bumps at the same time. Even when I was hunting, I didn't have reactions like this. But wasn't this the same, just the other side of the coin? The other side of the interaction? Hadn't I said something similar to men before? He was being straightforward, at least. Not vague. That was a plus. And maybe I would like his game, after all. The not knowing was intimidating, though.

I took a final swig of my tea and jumped down from the wall. "All right, hunter. Lead the way."

# Chapter Six

In the twenty-minute drive over to his house—I followed his BMW—I managed to talk myself out of the whole thing. I listed all the reasons that this was a bad idea: he made me crazy; we just about worked together; I wasn't interested in a relationship; I didn't have time for a relationship; plus, he made me crazy. This was just not a good idea.

We pulled into the driveway of a modest single-story ranch with a well-manicured lawn—at least as far as I could see in the dark. Somehow, I'd expected something more elaborate or flamboyant from an architect.

As I put the car into Park, I steeled myself to tell Evan that I'd changed my mind. I wasn't sure whether he'd understand. I didn't know whether I understood, really. I'd never gotten cold feet before.

I'd sat there long enough, apparently, for Evan to get out of his car and come to my door. I rolled the window down.

"You should stay," he said. Like he knew I was going to bail.

"I don't know."

"You're already here. If you'd really prefer not to be here, that is fine. But if you're just worried about how you're reacting, or if you're afraid of how you'll feel, consider whether that's something you want to rule your decisions." Illumination from the street lit his face. His expression was open, not guarded. "I'm going inside. I'll leave the door open in case you choose to join me. I hope that you do. It's an interesting conversation we've been having."

Choices. He kept giving me choices.

I sat in the car for a good ten minutes. At least it felt that long. It could have been shorter. I turned the engine off. Then on again. Then off. I looked at the sky—slightly overcast, but with a half-moon. I looked at my phone. There was another voice mail. The missed-call log showed it was Thomas. He was a nice guy. But if I was honest with myself—which I usually am but apparently not about Evan—I didn't find Thomas very intriguing. He would make a good catch for some woman. Just probably not me.

I sucked in a breath, tossed my phone into my purse, and turned the car on long enough to roll the window up. "All right, Caly. This doesn't have to be any different than taking a man home. It's just a different location." I popped the door open, got out, and closed it behind me. Then I took the driveway up to the side door that Evan had used.

I was in a smallish kitchen with stainless-steel appliances and marble countertops. Silver pots and pans lined the top of one wall. A blond-wood bistro table with matching chairs nestled in the corner. I closed the door behind me.

"I'm in the living room."

*Please let him not be in some smarmy smoking jacket and playing Barry White on the stereo.*

He wasn't. I tried not to sigh with relief. He hadn't changed clothes, and stood near a small bar in the corner. "I was just making myself a drink. Would you like something? I don't know how to make a lemon-drop martini, but I may have something else you'd like. Amaretto?"

"Amaretto is good." The living room was decorated in a modern way, with dark brown leather furniture and cherrywood accents. Sheers on the windows and light-colored paint on the walls. A chair rail bisecting all the way around.

"Please sit and relax. Do you want it on the rocks?"

"That's fine." I set my purse on the coffee table and settled onto the sofa. I sank back into the leather; it was a lot more comfortable than I expected. The clink of the ice into a glass brought my attention back to Evan. His T-shirt spanned broad shoulders and hugged his chest, loosening over his middle. There was a quarter-sized stain near the bottom, likely from something that splashed him at the shelter. When he turned to get the bottle of amaretto, I got a great view of a sexy jean-encased ass. Tightness gathered in my belly. The promise of this sort of view was what had caused me to approach Evan that very first night, I had to admit. He was definitely hotter than hot.

He handed me a short glass filled with ice and thick amber liquid. "I am glad you decided to come in." He sat on the sofa beside me but left enough room that I didn't feel crowded.

"So...the conversation we started at the shelter," I said. "I'd like you to talk more about it." The amaretto was sweet and smooth going down. I felt strangely stoic.

"My game, I assume you mean."

"Yes."

He leaned against the sofa, and I could almost see him thinking. After a long moment, he set his glass down and reached for mine. "I will show you, if you're willing."

*That word again.*

I let him take my drink and set it beside his on the coffee table. He took my hands and stood, so I rose with him. We went to the middle of the room. He stepped back and looked at me as he unfastened his belt. My heart raced.

What is he doing?

Uncertainty tingled along my skin, and my heartbeat hammered loud in my ears. He looked a trifle amused as he slid the belt out of his loops. It made a soft *snick*. He met my gaze. "Are you afraid?"

"I…I don't know." And that was true.

"I won't hurt you. I am just giving you a taste, so you have some understanding."

While his words were a relief, I hadn't come down from the edgy hyperawareness that had been growing since he had reached for his belt.

He draped the belt over his neck and then moved behind me. His hands warmed my wrists as he drew them behind my back and crossed one over the other. The leather of the belt was a cool contrast against my skin. He tightened the belt around my wrists and then shifted again to my front.

"The belt isn't firm. You can get out at any point. But I hope you trust me enough not to." His eyes searched mine, and I realized that there was a heavy feeling in my belly. My nipples tightened and pressed hard against my bra. He reached a hand up, and his fingers closed my eyes, his touch light like a feather. "Please keep them closed."

I took in shallow breaths, and my pussy flooded. I couldn't remember having been this turned on over nothing.

With my eyes closed, I lost visual input, but I could still hear him move around me. He stepped to my right, and I felt his body heat very close to my arm. Breath blew against the side of my neck, my ear. It was warm and then cool, tinged with the scent of whiskey. I shivered, and goose bumps tightened on my skin.

Something feathered against my other ear—a fingertip, maybe. And then my collarbones. He must have moved in front of me, because the light touch went along my shoulders and then down both arms at the same time, to my elbows. It was like little pulses of energy shot along my skin as his fingers moved.

I tried to keep my eyes closed but couldn't. And when I opened them, he stood inches from my nose, watching my face.

I wanted to run and I wanted to stay, at the same time. Vulnerability was never something I was good at, and now wasn't any different. I felt exposed. Almost raw. He stared at me with an open expression. No smugness; no arrogance. His attention didn't waver, and he seemed completely engrossed.

His gaze met mine, and the corner of his mouth perked upward. "You're not very good at following direction."

"I—"

He put a finger on my lips, and the dimple appeared. "Don't worry." He closed my eyes again the same way he had before, and I felt his heat as he leaned close to my ear and spoke in a soft, clear, firm tone. "Keep them closed."

I couldn't stop the shiver from running down my spine. I wasn't used to being the one who was bossed around. I was usually the one in control. I flexed my fingers and felt a little give in the belt. Knowing I could shake my hands and it would likely fall to the ground kept me from freaking out. But I knew I wouldn't do it. This was weird, a little uncomfortable, but everything in me was tuned in to him right now. And, I had to admit, I liked it.

His scent enveloped me—sweet, with that slight undercurrent of alcohol—and I felt his presence so close. A moment later, his chest brushed against me, against my breasts. A part of me—the part that was always assessing things around me—wondered if he felt the hardness of my nipples through my shirt and bra.

His hands ran over my exposed skin, more than fingertips this time. His whole palm. I kept expecting him to squeeze my breast or try to lift my T-shirt, but he never did. The heat from his hands left trails of fire across me. My breathing came in short, quick gasps.

In the darkness behind my eyes, everything felt more intense, more immediate. He leaned in, and again his breath traveled over my skin—my face this time—and stubble from his cheek brushed against my own cheek. Fingertips traced the shells of my ears, and another shiver rode my spine. I think my body actually shook from it.

He moved to my side, his chest rubbing against my arm as he continued all the way around behind me. He grasped my upper arms tightly and pushed his body into mine from the back. His sweet scent invaded me. I leaned into him, and one of his arms came around my shoulders. He pinned me to him and tilted back. I flowed with him. I relaxed into his hold. I didn't think he would drop me, and I had no other choice, really.

We angled forward again as one, and then he straightened. His breath at my ear and then, "Good."

Cool air brushed against me as he stepped away and released his hold. I had to keep from moving back with him; I missed his touch already. The belt slid from my wrists, and I heard him slipping it back into his loops. I kept my hands where they were and my eyes closed.

His buckle clinked as he fastened it, and then I felt his heat move to the front of me. He touched my left temple and said, "Open."

I had never noticed that his irises, already brown, were ringed with a much darker brown. I noticed them now. I blinked against the light of the room, which had seemed dim before, but now seemed bright as noon.

He smiled at me, a soft, gentle smile. "You see? Different rules. Different game." He motioned the sofa, as if we could resume where we'd left off before this flight of fancy.

My mind had gone blank. I tried to process what had just happened, but it wasn't coming. I moved to the sofa in a haze and sat back down. He joined me where he'd sat before and lifted both our glasses from the table. He handed me my amaretto. I stared at the glass, and it took me a moment to remember what to do with it. When I did, I took a sip. The flavor seemed brighter, bolder, sweeter.

I raked my gaze up his body to his face. I had no words.

And he gave me no words. We sat in silence for a long time. At least, it seemed like a long time.

Finally, he said, "Do you work at the shelter tomorrow?"

"I'm sorry?"

A small uptick at the corner of his mouth. "Are you going to Helping Hands tomorrow to work?"

"Oh. Yes. I'd planned to."

"Do you mind if I go again, as well?"

Did I mind? Was it my place to mind? It wasn't like we didn't always need more help at the shelter. "There's more than enough to do." I was glad my brain was working, even if it was at limited capacity.

"That isn't what I asked." Evan raised his glass to his lips and looked at me over the top as he took a drink.

"Are you asking my permission?"

"No. I am asking for your feelings on the matter."

*Oh.* "If you want to help out, I am fine with that."

He didn't respond right away, only continued to look at me. I suddenly wondered if that wasn't the answer he was looking for.

"I will likely ask you to do something for me tomorrow. You are under no obligation to do it, of course. But I would like it if you did."

My guard rose. So here it was. Kinky sex. "I am not going to give you a blowjob at the shelter."

His eyebrows rose, and then he laughed—a full-throated, deep rumble. "No. No, you're not."

Heat rose on my skin. Okay, obviously that wasn't what he meant. So what else was there to ask? "What do you want then?"

He stood and took my now empty glass. I didn't remember drinking the rest. "Tomorrow." He disappeared into the kitchen, and I sat back into the sofa, surrounded by the feel of leather.

A hall on the other side of the room probably led to the bedrooms. I'd come here thinking we were going to have sex, and now I wondered if that would happen at all. And whether I was disappointed if it didn't.

When Evan returned, he glanced at his watch. "It's been a long day. We should probably both call it a night."

*Seriously?* I stood. "Are you joking?"

He tilted his head and raised one brow. "No. It hasn't been a long day for you?" I couldn't tell whether he was mocking me or being serious.

But he was right. It had been a really long day. But I wasn't going to give him the satisfaction of agreement.

When it was obvious I wasn't going to respond, he broke into that whole-face grin again. "See? Different game."

He held out a hand toward the door in that universal gesture of *come, young lady, it's time for you to be moving along.*

I was being dismissed. How did he always seem to be perfectly charming and lovely, and then all of a sudden he became the biggest asshole in all existence? I would have to ask him that another time, when I wasn't fuming.

Very slowly and deliberately, I reached down and grabbed my purse. I wasn't going to let him see that he'd pissed me off. "Thank you for the drink." I moved toward the door, and just as I stepped past him, his finger and thumb touched my elbow. I stopped and turned my head to look at him.

His hand came up, and the tip of his forefinger touched my chin with a feather of pressure. His scent enveloped me, and heat gathered in my belly. Again. He leaned down to my ear. On a breath that tickled my skin, he said, "Thank you." Then he kissed me. Not aggressive. No tongue. He just brushed his lips over mine so I barely felt their silky texture.

When he pulled away, it was a struggle not to lean forward. I wanted more. But his hand was on the small of my back now, and he guided me to the door. I don't remember what he said by way of good-bye, but I walked, robotic, to my car. I got in, started the engine, and apparently made it home fine. But I don't really remember that either.

--->>><<<---

Saturday morning went by in a blur. I ran a lot of errands, but my mind wasn't in it. I went everywhere and got everything I was supposed to, but I couldn't keep from going back to the night before: the belt around my wrists, the touches, the kiss. Every time I thought of the kiss, I shivered. It hadn't even been one of those earth-shattering, quivers-to-the-tips-of-my-toes sort of kiss. It had been gentle and almost chaste. But just thinking of it woke my body up.

And then there was the thing he was going to ask me to do tonight. That made me shiver too. The anticipation, the not knowing. Every time I tried to envision what it might be, I came up blank.

I was letting myself into the apartment, trying to balance half a dozen bags, so I could grab a shower and change before heading to the shelter, when my phone rang. It played some angry-girl music, which was my default ringtone, so I knew it wasn't anyone superimportant. I managed to get inside with only dropping one bag—luckily it had clothes in it and not eggs. Once I'd rescued everything onto the kitchen counter, I checked my phone.

Thomas.

I hadn't thought about him once all day. I tried to remember if I owed him a phone call. I thought I might. He left a message, but I decided not to listen to it yet. I set my phone aside and put away the three bags of groceries and three bags of miscellaneous stuff, including a new short-sleeved light sweater that I bought to wear tonight. And that was pretty dumb. Who wore a new sweater to work in a homeless shelter?

Luckily, by the time I'd showered and gotten ready to head over, my rational mind had reengaged. I wore jeans and my way-too-big Helping Hands T-shirt. I'd won it in a raffle fund-raiser two years ago. It was comfy, even though it was two sizes too big. Right now, I was so off-kilter on the inside, comfort on the outside seemed like the best idea ever.

Apparently, I'd been staving off nerves all day, but as I drove over to Helping Hands, my stomach got all fluttery. I was caught between chiding myself for being so goofy and laughing at myself for the same reason. I never felt this way when I hunted guys to take home. I didn't know if it was something about Evan particularly or simply this time being…prey. *Ugh.* I didn't like that word. It seemed weak.

I pushed that from my mind and drove the rest of the way trying to anticipate what Evan would ask me to do. That was a pretty fruitless line of thought, though. I had no idea.

The small lot beside the shelter was almost empty. I saw Annette and Jessie's old minivan and a modest, late-model sedan that I thought belonged to one of the new volunteers who had started coming out after the big fund-raisers earlier in the year. I parked, stashed my purse in my trunk, and went in.

I got hellos from a number of the shelter residents and regulars. I stopped to chat and check on how things were going with them—one of the young mothers had gotten a job!—and then went on to the kitchen where I found Jessie at the helm of the Great Lasagna Bake-Off. We did lasagna about twice a month, and it was always a big production, because we didn't just buy huge pans of frozen food. Jessie stayed away from processed food whenever she could. She always said that our guests' lives were crappy enough; they didn't need to be eating bad food too. So the lasagna was made from scratch. Well, not the noodles. But everything else...

I washed my hands at the white porcelain sink attached to the wall and then went to Jessie at the stove. "What do you need me to do?"

"Here." She handed me the spatula. "Finish up the meat? I think there's four packages left. I've already done two." She motioned to the huge packs of ground beef and then at the big but mostly empty bowl of already browned meat.

Okay, this was going to take a while. "Sure. No problem."

"Great! Annette should be back with the produce, so I'm going to have to get on chopping up tomatoes and I need to do a couple office-y things." It cracked me up when she made up words. Jessie always seemed so proper.

So she went off, and I kept up with the beef browning. Spices lined the counter behind the packages, and each time I did a new batch, I salted, peppered, and Italian spiced it. I found myself taking constant peeks into the dining area to see if Evan had arrived—he hadn't—and then still constantly wondering what was in store for me.

—➤➤◄◄◄—

When he did finally arrive, I was cutting up loaves for garlic bread. I didn't even realize he was there until he came up behind me and said, "Good wardrobe choice."

I whirled around, my heart thumping. "God, you scared me."

"My apologies. I didn't mean to." He wore jeans again, but this time with a gray ringer T-shirt. It wasn't tight, but formfitting enough to see his shape: broad shoulders, strong arms, a bit of a belly, but not much.

Adrenaline had spiked in my system, but I managed to get my breathing back under control after he startled me. "You should be more careful about scaring people who are holding sharp knives." I waved it around for emphasis.

"Excellent suggestion and so noted. When did you get here?"

"A couple hours ago." I turned back to the counter and continued to cut bread.

"You spend all day here."

"Just about."

He came closer and leaned against the counter. "For as much as you portray being a hardass, I think you're one of those people who has the proverbial heart of gold."

I tried not to blush, but heat suffused my cheeks. "Things need to be done. That's all." Subject change. "Has Jessie given you anything to do?"

"I haven't seen her yet. I'll go find her in a second. I just wanted to thank you for stopping over last night. I enjoyed our time together."

What did that mean, exactly? I wanted to take it at face value, but was this part of his game? I didn't know. "You said you wanted me to do something?" I didn't pause in my slicing. I didn't want him to think I cared as much as I did.

"Yes. But later. After everything's ready for dinner, but before service."

I looked at him, and he was smiling. It seemed like his genuine smile. I was getting that much more than I was getting his smirking or snarky smiles lately. I sort of liked it.

"All right." Even though I was dying to know what it was, I wasn't going to ask. "You should probably go find Jessie, then. She was heading out in the dining room to chop tomatoes last time I saw her."

He pushed himself off the counter. "Will do."

I tried not to turn around and stare at his ass as he left.

I failed.

# Chapter Seven

As we got things ready for dinner, I got more and more nervous. I babbled whenever anyone asked me something. I dropped utensils on the floor. I almost tripped twice just walking across the kitchen floor. I was basically a klutzy mess. And that was annoying, because normally I'm not a klutz at all.

Finally, we'd gotten to a point where the lasagne were done and setting for fifteen minutes while the garlic bread was in the oven. Someone else was laying out greens for the salad, and all the veggies had been chopped or put in bowls. Dessert was ready—lemon custard pudding with whipped cream—and things settled down for a few minutes before the doors opened.

Evan approached with something in his hand hidden by holding it behind his wrist. My skin was tight and hot all over as soon as I saw him. Maybe this wasn't such a good idea.

"Ready?" He put a hand on my elbow.

"I'm not sure."

"It's all right. If you change your mind, that is fine. Let's go into the office for a minute."

I almost panicked. Did Jessie and Annette know what was going on?

But when we got to the office, it was empty. We stepped inside, and he closed the door behind us.

It was just a small room—I think it had been a supply closet in another lifetime—with two desks crammed against perpendicular walls. It was decorated in Classic New Age, with hippy posters and crystals. Jessie even had a framed photo of her with Jimi Hendrix. Apparently, they'd been a thing for a while back in the day.

The click of the lock catching jerked me into the present. I turned and faced him. His expression was passive but not distant.

"I told you I would ask you to do something today."

"Yes."

"What I am going to ask you to do is wear something for me. Are you willing to do that?"

"It's not crotchless underwear, is it?" Even coming out of my mouth, that sounded crass, and I cringed on the inside. I tried to temper it with a grin, but I knew it came across as weak. For his part, Evan just looked amused. As usual, I supposed.

"No, it is not crotchless underwear."

"Oh good."

"Will you take off your T-shirt for a moment?"

"Umm." Okay, that was not expected. "I guess I can."

"I am positive that you can. I am asking if you will." I searched his face to see if he was being snarky, but I couldn't find any sense of condescension or smart-assy-ness.

"Can I ask why?" I wasn't being snarky either.

"Because what I would like for you to wear should be worn underneath. I suppose I could put it on top of your shirt, but you'd likely have to answer a question or two if I did." The boyish grin that spread across his face made my pulse speed up—as usual. And it made my pussy tingle—again, as usual.

"All right." I closed my eyes and lifted my shirt over my head. I hadn't worn a sexy bra—who does that when they're going to work in a kitchen?—but at least it wasn't a ratty one.

He took my shirt from me and laid it over the back of Annette's chair. "Hands on your head, please." I tried not to think about my fat arms. I suddenly felt even more vulnerable.

As I did what he asked, he finally brought out what he'd been holding this whole time. A coil of rope. It reminded me of rope I'd seen when I'd gone boating in the Caribbean during the summer between my sophomore and junior years of undergrad. But it wasn't as big. It was dark tan and pretty thin.

This was what all the buildup was about? I'd thought it was going to be something exciting.

He unfastened an end of the coil and let the remaining rope drop to the floor with a *thunk*. It had been folded in half before it was coiled, apparently, because the end he held in his hand now was the little loop of the fold.

He moved close and reached both arms around me slowly, almost like a hug. His nose wasn't two inches from mine, and he kept my gaze as his arms wrapped around me. His sweet and spicy scent surrounded us both, and I breathed it in. He spread the doubled-up rope around my torso, just above my breasts. He took one step back and returned his attention to the rope. He fed the loose ends into the loop of the fold and pulled it all the way through, forming a wrap around my chest.

The grassy smell of the strands mingled with Evan's scent, and it was almost intoxicating. The rope hugged my body as Evan tightened it. He ran his fingers under the wrap around my chest, fiddling with it, straightening it. Then he shifted the entire thing so the folded bit was beneath my arm. The rope scratched along my skin, waking up all my nerve endings. He reversed his direction and ran the next line directly beneath the first one, all the way around.

He watched what he was doing so intently. When he got back to the beginning, which was now below my arm, he ran the rope through more than once—tying it off?—and then he did another wrap, but below my breasts. He didn't touch me except to adjust the rope. And I found that I wanted him to. Touch me, that is.

I realized I had been arching my back just a little bit, which caused my breasts to thrust out. I flushed when I realized that I was doing it, and I tried to relax my posture without calling attention to myself. I should have known better. He was in front of me when I did and, though he didn't say anything, his gaze rose to meet mine and the corner of his mouth ticked up. Then he continued to move around me, guiding the rope against my body.

With every wrap, I felt more tightly held. Not to the point of discomfort, but enough to know that the rope was there. When he finished the second wrap below my breasts, he said, "Take a deep breath."

I filled my lungs as full as I could, which was actually a little bit less than normal. I couldn't quite get an entire lungful, but very close.

"Is that okay? You can breathe?"

"Yes. It's fine."

He pulled the rope through a couple more times, and then he stepped back. "You can lower your arms now."

When I did, the rope felt tighter, like a gentle cocoon.

"Deep breath."

I wasn't able to fill my lungs quite as much as before, but it was still okay.

"Light-headed? Feeling weird?" He studied my face as he spoke.

"No. I mean, it's a little harder to breathe, but not bad. I feel okay."

"Good." He lifted my shirt from the chair and handed it to me. "Thank you for wearing my rope."

I pulled the shirt over my head. "Um. You're welcome, I guess." He never even copped a feel. "I thought it was going to be something big."

His humor sparkled in his eyes. "It is."

My belly quivered. I wondered if this was how my men felt when I was hunting them. "Is that it?"

"Yep."

"We go back out there now?"

"Yes, and work the service as normal. If you do find yourself feeling light-headed at all during the evening, come to me right away." The intensity of his gaze bored into me. "Yes?"

I nodded. I couldn't find my voice just then. I couldn't even have put into words what I was feeling.

"I'd like you to come to my house after, and we will take it off there. Perhaps add more before we take it off, if you wish."

I wasn't sure how to answer. I wasn't sure it was actually a question. And I also wasn't sure if I had my words back yet. So I didn't say anything at all, just unlocked the office door and pulled it open. It suddenly occurred to me that I should probably have checked to see if anyone was around to witness us leaving the office together, but I couldn't say my mind classified that as important right at that moment.

I found myself preoccupied with the tightness around my chest. The scent of the rope and Evan's body lingered on me. I only barely registered all the volunteers heading to the kitchen. Annette did a nightly combination pep and thank-you talk before dinner for the volunteers. She found it important to express her gratitude. I usually skipped them, but this time I followed Evan into the back.

Turned out that I still skipped it, because nothing she said really made it into my head until she singled Evan out. She praised him for designing the new building and in putting his hard work where his mouth was by also contributing his labor this weekend. Evan only smiled and nodded. I couldn't say exactly what made me think so, but he seemed to be a bit bothered by the attention.

Finally, Annette released us for our duties. Evan would be working behind the lines, replenishing bread and salad, cutting the new trays of lasagna for those on the line to portion out. I was out in the dining room again, helping with cleanup, drinks, and whatever else was necessary. Weekends were always a lot busier than during the week. A number of our homeless folks actually did hold down jobs, so sometimes during the week they ate elsewhere. But most were here for the weekends.

Before we went our separate ways for the evening service, Evan touched my elbow. "Still feeling okay?"

His words were very earnest, so I paused a second to actually assess, rather than just saying I was fine. I did feel constrained, but not overly so. I took a breath. I couldn't expand my chest fully, but I could breathe deep enough for comfort. "Yes. I'm good."

The look he gave me sent a tingle from my head to my toes. "Excellent," he said. "I will see you after service, then."

I nodded and then headed to the dining room. As I moved about my duties, straightening the condiment table, checking the garbage cans, wiping down tables, I realized that a low arousal bubbled just beneath the surface. Every time I moved, the rope rubbed against my skin, holding me tight. Sometimes I would catch the scent and that would remind me of Evan's hands not quite on me as he applied the rope. So during the entire dinner, my pussy did a constant, low thrum and the fabric of my bra scraped against my pebbled nipples. By the end of the evening, I wanted to go into the bathroom and rub one out. All my nerves were on edge.

I caught Evan watching me every so often. I smiled at him more than once and he returned each one. When all the cleanup was done and my good-byes were said, Evan walked out to the parking lot with me.

"Will you come to my house?"

"For more…" I motioned my torso.

"I would like that, yes. If you'd prefer, I can simply take it off here, in the car."

I tried very hard not to decide with my pussy, but it was pretty adamant that I go with him. In the end, I liked the rope. I liked Evan putting it on. And I was interested in seeing what else there was to this. "All right. Lead the way."

---

I was excited during the entire trip until we pulled into his driveway. Then I got nervous. Not because I was afraid for my safety, but because I had no idea what would happen when I walked through that door. It was a punch in the gut reminder that I am not used to not being in control. It was incredibly uncomfortable.

Evan stood beside his car, watching me, obviously waiting for me to get out. Again. Even though I held the handle, I had trouble pulling it to open the door. He walked to me and paused. When I still didn't open the door, he did.

"Will you come in?" There was no pressure in the words. It seemed a simple question.

"I want to."

He didn't laugh, but he looked...not really amused. More delighted. His eyes glittered in the light from the street. He held out his hand as if I were a lady in a carriage. "May I help you?"

His skin was cool when I slipped my hand into his. "Thank you." For his hand. For calming my nerves. For understanding. I couldn't be sure he *actually* understood. But I suspected he did. I still had trouble reconciling this Evan with the Evan of the snark and annoying habits. But I wondered if this Evan was more the real Evan. I hoped so.

He led me to the side door, released my hand, and pulled his keys from his pocket. When we got inside, the kitchen smelled of tomatoes and oregano. I took a deep breath.

"I made pasta sauce today. Apparently, it's Italian day everywhere." He shot me a wink as he closed the door. He ushered me into the living room, which looked exactly as it had the night before. "Amaretto?"

"Thank you." Perhaps the liqueur would take the edge off a little bit.

I felt the rope even more distinctly now that I was here in his house. As I sat on the sofa, I fancied that I could feel each individual wrap pressed against my skin, and I imagined I felt the weave of the rope move against me as I breathed. What would happen next? What else could he do with rope? I shivered. And I didn't even know what I was shivering about.

Evan handed me a short glass with a couple ice cubes and amaretto. "Are you cold?"

"No, not really."

He touched my wrist briefly, and it felt reassuring. "Nerves?"

"Probably."

"Nothing to be nervous about."

"So the rope thing is part of your game."

"Yes." He settled onto the sofa beside me. "There are lots of parts, and that is one."

"What are the other parts?" I met his gaze directly, and he kept it for a moment before responding.

"I enjoy control, so most of the game that I play has to do with that."

"Control? Like bossing someone around."

"That is one aspect, yes. Or knowing they wear my rope beneath their clothes. That gives me a measure of control over how they are feeling." He tilted his head toward me and his eyes glimmered with humor. "Did you feel differently wearing my rope?"

"Yes." I was not going to tell him about wanting to run into the bathroom and get myself off. "My awareness seemed heightened."

"That will happen."

I didn't know what else to say, so I sipped my drink. I didn't really taste it, though. My nerves sat on edge; I hadn't felt this crazy and uncertain in the presence of a man in years and years. High school probably. Not even the other interactions we'd had had come to this level.

"Would you like more?"

I looked at my drink. Did he mean amaretto?

He laughed, light and airy. "Rope. Would you like more rope?" He lifted my chin with a finger until I met his gaze. My skin broke out into goose bumps, and his touch sent a tingle straight to my pussy. "You are really out of your element, aren't you? You're not used to this."

I struggled against anger. I knew it was irrational. I knew it came from being off my footing and uncomfortable and from him recognizing that I was off my footing and uncomfortable. I shifted my head away from his finger. "What does 'more rope' entail?"

He dropped his hand and looked at me for a long time. "I had actually intended to literally put more rope on you. But I think, now, I want to do something different. I'd like to take off what you have on and then… I don't know that I can explain it, but it doesn't involve binding you, so much as it involves us experiencing rope very intimately, together."

I tried to figure out what that meant. "Sex and rope?"

"No." He lifted a shoulder in a half shrug. "Well, I suppose by the description, it could be that, but that's not my intention at this time. There is a style of rope called Ichinawa. It only involves one rope. I think I would like to do it with you."

I had no idea what made that any different from any other rope thing. I wondered at how involved he was in…whatever it was he was involved in. "Is this that *Fifty Shades* thing?"

A sharp, sudden laugh erupted from him. "Sort of. But this is real and not a fantasy." It sounded as if he had more to say on the topic, but he didn't share.

"Does it involve spanking and all that?"

"It can."

"It can for you, or in general?"

"Both."

"Oh."

Silence hung in the air for a minute. I'd heard of kink and BDSM, of course. No one who spends any time on the Internet could possibly avoid it. But it had never really occurred to me to try it. Sure, I liked being in control when I was hunting, but I never did any of the beat-me stuff. That was never my thing. And the leather and cuffs seemed like a lot of work. I just wanted to make sure the encounter went my way. This…this was entirely different. But whether it was the kink or just Evan's presence, I couldn't deny the heavy feeling in my belly and my inclination to kiss him.

"Will you allow me to take my rope off you?"

I nodded.

He took both our drinks and set them on the coffee table and then rose and offered his hand to me again. I took it, and he led me to the middle of the living room. "Your shirt, please."

*Oh yeah.* I pulled it over my head. The rope moved with me as I did. I felt a weird pang of melancholy. It would be gone soon. He took my tee from me and laid it on the arm of the sofa. I put my hands on my head and again tried not to think about my fat arms flapping in the wind. It felt like déjà vu.

"Good girl."

I froze. The independent woman in me warred with my libido. The former wanted to punch him for being a misogynistic asshole—was he a misogynistic asshole? The latter wanted to jump his bones and fuck him silly. How did those two things live in me side by side?

My thoughts were halted by his hands on me. He placed each hand flat against my skin, one on my belly, just below the rope and my breasts, the other on my back in the same place. He pushed them together, a light pressure. A controlling pressure. Then he released me and set to work on the rope.

I watched him in my peripheral vision as he took the rope off. He moved with such fluidity. His arms came out in long sweeps as he pulled the rope through. As the wraps came loose, he would toss the long end around me and catch it in the hand behind my back. Before I knew it, all the rope was gone.

I felt cold. Almost naked. It was strange.

He dropped the rope onto the floor and opened his arms to me. I stepped into the circle of them, and his warmth wrapped around me to replace the rope. His scent permeated my everything. He held me there for what felt like a long time. Finally he leaned back, looked at me, and said, "I would like to do more rope. Will you do that with me?"

I wanted to ask a bunch of questions about what it would look like, what we would do. But I felt relaxed, and I realized I didn't want to expend the energy on asking. "Yes."

He gave me warm fuzzies. I didn't know what it was about him, but he was definitely under my skin. I still didn't know what that meant.

"My preference is no clothes for you. But I am fine with whatever you are comfortable with. I am going to get my rope kit. You can decide what you'd like to do about clothing and let me know when I return." He stepped away from me, and I felt cold again, but not as bad as when the rope first came off. I wrapped my hands around myself and watched him disappear down the hall.

Did I want to get naked? I didn't think so. That was too much vulnerability. Too much skin showing. I'd already struggled with my arms. I didn't think I could handle that level of accessibility right now. If we were just fucking, sure. But I didn't even know what we were going to be doing. Not really. And already this seemed way more intimate than just fucking. I tried to work out whether that was weird or not—that I was okay getting naked to fuck, but not to do rope—but decided, again, I didn't want to spend the time or energy on it.

He returned with a canvas bag in his hand. It was about the size of a backpack and seemed to be stuffed full. "Have you decided?"

"Yes. I don't think I am ready for no clothes. I am okay with stripping down to panties and bra, though." I waited for him to balk, or say that I was being silly.

"That's fine."

"Really?"

His brow furrowed just a little. "Yes, really. I told you that whatever you decide would be fine."

"I know. I thought you might be disappointed, though."

He grinned and set the bag on the arm of the sofa. "Well, yeah, I am. But it's a small disappointment, in the grand scheme of things. And being disappointed a little bit certainly isn't the end of the world. You're still willing to do rope with me. That's the important part." He opened the bag and began to pull out coils of rope. The piece he'd put on me at the shelter had been natural color, but he had a rainbow in his bag. There was blue and green, red and black, even purple. I didn't realize rope came in those colors.

"I am thinking red. Do you have a preference?"

"Are they different from each other besides color?"

"No. They are all jute. Some are older and so a little softer, but overall, they're the same." He picked up a remote control, pressed a couple buttons, and soft classical music drifted into the air.

"Then red is fine."

"Excellent."

"Should I take off my pants now?" It was weird not knowing what to expect. Things were starting to feel surreal.

Evan hiked his shirt over his head and said, "That would be a good idea. And also, quid pro quo. You're down to skivvies, so I will be down to skivvies." A dark dusting of curly hair covered his chest, thickest between his pecs. The ridges and slopes of his muscles were apparent, though not defined like a weight lifter's. I tried not to stare. A zing of desire shot through me as he unbuttoned his jeans.

I mirrored his move with my jeans and slid them down my hips. I was glad I'd worn lace panties, even if I hadn't thought ahead to wearing a matching set. At least I hadn't gone for my too-lazy-to-care cotton granny panties. Thank goodness for small favors.

As I folded my jeans, I snuck a peek at Evan, who'd already shimmied out of his and tossed them on the sofa. He wore black boxer briefs that hugged his ass like I would want to hug his ass. He had thick, muscled thighs and strong-looking calves.

I suddenly felt huge.

"Do you go to the gym?" I asked.

He had moved to a hall closet and pulled out a soft-looking throw blanket. "Not often, no." He flipped a couple light switches and slid a dimmer. The room darkened, but only a bit. Like dusk.

"I just wondered because you look like you're in really good shape."

"I'm a martial artist. I'm at the dojo several times a week, and I run when I can't get there." He returned to the middle of the room and spread the throw on the floor. He took a coil of the red rope and dropped it at the corner of the blanket. Then he turned to me with that smile. "Ready?"

I laughed, and it sounded strained even to me. "I guess. I'm not sure what I'm ready for."

"You'll be fine. Don't worry." He took my hand and brought me onto the blanket. Its softness cushioned the bottoms of my feet. "Can you kneel?"

"Not for a long amount of time." I'd fucked my knee up in a winter fall on my parents' steps several years ago.

"That's fine. I'll shift you after a bit. In the center, please."

I moved as he asked and knelt in the middle of the throw. He came behind me and got to his knees also, his thighs outside mine. He must not have been kneeling down, though, because he was still taller. His heat radiated onto my back, though he wasn't quite close enough to touch me.

He touched a finger to the front of my temple. "Closed, please."

I shut my eyes and took a long, deep breath. As I finished the breath, he leaned forward, against my back, and wrapped his arms around my torso, just below my breasts. Then *he* took a long, deep breath. His chest pushed into my back as he expanded his lungs. His chest hair raked along the skin of my back. As he released, I realized I was releasing a breath as well. He breathed in again. I breathed in. Out. Out. In. In. He held me tight as we breathed together. I found my anxiety slipping away as I breathed there, in the dark with him.

He took my left arm and raised it over and just behind my head, then put pressure on my forearm, urging toward my right shoulder. My muscle tightened with the movement. He held it for several seconds, then gently lowered my arm. He did the same with my right arm, angling it over my head and to the left. I felt the stretch in my triceps. Was that what he was doing? Stretching me? That seemed odd.

He slid his arm through my elbow toward my back and pulled my arm against his chest. My shoulder muscles stretched. And then he did the same on the other side. The whole while he continued to breathe, pausing to press his chest against my back, which made me breathe in time with him. He wrapped his arms around me again and hugged me tight to him. We rocked forward and back for a long moment. Everything—his movement, his scent, just his presence—soothed me, and I felt more relaxed than I had in a very long time.

He remained against me, but let his hands roam over my skin. His palms skimmed my arms and my belly—I tried hard not to be self-conscious. He rested his chin on my shoulder as he moved his hands down across the outsides of my thighs. His breath tickled along my neck and collarbone. Then he wrapped around me again, and we rocked for a few moments more.

One of his arms left me briefly and then returned. Rope, a little bit scratchy and smelling of grass, rubbed against my shoulder, across my chest and up my neck. He hadn't uncoiled it. It felt like a big lump of rope. His arms moved again, and I heard the rustle of rope on rope. Then a strand—double strand?—fell across my thighs. He dragged it slowly and it tickled my skin as it moved. He drew the piece up over my breasts and over my shoulder, the whole thing trailing lightly over my skin.

My entire body woke up. My skin received every touch from the rope or from him with a jolt of electricity. As he ran the strand behind my neck and down my other shoulder, goose bumps broke out and I shivered. My breathing had quickened, and the low moan from my throat surprised me.

His hand trailed down my left arm and grasped my wrist. He brought it close to my body, and I felt rope being wrapped around it. I peeked from beneath my lashes and saw him anchoring the rope around my wrist. I closed my eyes again. I didn't really need to see. I'd realized that this wasn't about seeing.

Using the long end of the rope, he brought my wrist up to my right shoulder, positioning my arm across my chest. He pulled the rope down my back, across and around the left side of my torso. He made it tight, and the rope bit into my skin. It hurt but didn't, at the same time. He angled me back against him, and I leaned, letting my head roll back on his shoulder. His scent—cloves and sweetness—hit me again. I breathed deep.

He wrapped the rope around my arm and my belly from left to right. He pushed me forward with a hand in the middle of my back until I was leaning down, head almost to the floor. I felt him pull the free strand through the piece hugging my back, and then he pulled me up by the rope. It bit into my skin in the front, with painful little lines. I swayed into him again.

The rope came against the front of my neck, but gently, his thumb guiding it, brushing my skin back and forth. A little twinge of panic tried to overcome me, but I pushed it down. He was giving me sensation. He wasn't even tightening the rope. I relaxed again.

After that, things just became fuzzy. He unwound the rope from me, leaving the anchor on my wrist. Then my arm was drawn behind my back, and he wrapped the rope around my torso, binding my upper arm to my side and my wrist and hand to my back. He never tied the rope off. His palms roamed over my skin, warm and earnest. He left trails of heat wherever he touched.

He shoved my body forward again and then covered me with his. The weight of him held me down. I didn't feel fear, but rather comfort. His weight comforted me.

Surrounded. Cocooned. Safe.

My mind turned off, and I floated. His movements against me still registered, but only from a distance. I had no real concept of the order in which he did things. Nothing hurt. Everything felt good and right.

"You are beautiful in rope," he whispered very close to my ear.

I couldn't respond except a soft, wordless murmur.

He leaned me sideways, until I came onto my hip.

"Feet forward."

I straightened my legs, and the muscles unbunched, stretching out as I did.

"Good girl."

He released my wrist from the rope and then leaned forward, over me again, folding my body in half beneath him. His hands lifted one leg slightly, and the rope slid under, rubbing against the sensitive skin of my inner thigh as he anchored it there. The rope moved over my body, leaving trails of electricity and comfort. He wrapped me up once, twice and then again. It all ran together, and I settled into the feelings.

When he leaned me back against his chest and ran his hands over my shoulders, arms, breasts, and belly, I groaned, every nerve ending firing at once. I squirmed against him, and he raised me to sitting and unwound the rope, only to rewind it again, quickly, around my shoulders, folding me down again over my legs. His speed made my heart race, and all that electricity he generated went straight to my pussy. My entire body thrummed with desire. I'd never experienced anything like this before.

He pushed me onto my side. The rope went from my thigh, over my back, and then under the side I lay on. I felt tension in the rope—he still had the loose end. One of his knees aligned parallel with my back and ass, the other aligned with my thighs.

*He could fuck me in this position.*

That's what I wanted, more than anything at this moment. His cock in me, fucking me silly while I was in his rope. I tried to grind myself against him, but the position didn't work for that. He dropped down to all fours, his arms on either side of me. Caged.

His breath caressed my cheek, my ear, as he leaned close. "Not tonight."

I groaned again. I didn't mean to. But I did.

He dropped a soft kiss onto my shoulder and then hauled me up by the rope into a sitting position again. His movements had slowed down, sensual and gentle. His skin slid across mine as he reached around for the rope, and I imagined I could feel every one of his chest hairs individually. He untethered the anchor from my thigh, and I heard the rope hit the floor a foot or so away. And then his arms came around me from behind and he held me tight.

---

I didn't know how long we sat there, his arms around me. It felt like an hour. Maybe it was only a few minutes. But I floated, inside my head. I was never a big exercise buff, but it felt similar to an exercise high. But not quite the same. I didn't analyze it. I just enjoyed the feelings.

His body was warm, and it felt as if he'd worked up a little bit of a sweat. But he held me, and his warmth and smell made me safe. He rubbed a hand on my head, over my hair. He traced my edge of my ear—which made me shiver—and he planted a soft kiss on my temple.

Eventually, I found my words. "I have never had an experience like that before." And that was true.

"Did you enjoy it?"

"Yes." I didn't hesitate. There was no reason to. "But it was strange."

"Different," he said. "Foreign."

"Yes." Silence spread between us for a few moments, not uncomfortable. "How did you learn to do that?"

"It's taken me some time and a lot of practice. That isn't a particularly technical sort of thing, but being adept at handling rope makes the experience much more memorable."

I didn't really get what he was talking about, so I didn't respond. In truth, my brain was not functioning at peak capacity just then. I was fuzzy and only really grasping basics. That was okay, though.

"Are you ready to get up?"

I wasn't sure. So again, I didn't answer.

After a moment, he laughed. "I will take that as a no." And he squeezed me and brushed a hand over my hair again.

We lay there for a while longer, but eventually I was ready to move. He helped me to my feet, and I was surprised that I was unsteady. Not dizzy, exactly. But I found myself swaying. Apparently, this was normal, because Evan didn't let go of my arm until both of my feet were firmly grounded.

He helped me with my shirt, which cascaded down to my hips once we got it over my head.

"Can I just wait on the jeans for a few minutes?" I sat on the sofa.

"Of course."

And that's when I realized Evan hadn't put on his clothes yet either. And that his boxer briefs were tented…with a very steep tent. Or as steep as a tent could be with such tight-fitting clothing. "I can… I can help you with that." I raised my gaze to his.

He had that little smile. Not the full one. Not the snarky one. The small one that seemed to say he was both amused and happy. "Not tonight, Caly. Sometime, yes, if you are willing. But not tonight." He bent and picked up the rope.

I tried not to feel rejected, because he did seem as if he was interested. But it was still a blow to my female ego. "Why not tonight?"

He held the rope in both hands and began to coil it. I was again struck by his grace. "Because tonight was about giving you an experience. I will have my experience another night." He tipped a wink at me, and that made me laugh.

"You seem very sure of yourself."

He tilted his head but didn't reply as he finished off the coil. He dropped the bundle onto his bag, then came over and sat on the sofa beside me. He leaned back and held one arm wide. I shifted so that I could press into him, and he wrapped me up in his strength.

"Thank you," he said.

"For what? You're the one who did the work."

"For allowing me to tie you. You trusted me enough to go into something with only the barest knowledge of what would happen. I appreciate that honor."

Again—and apparently, as usual—I didn't know what to say. So I said, "You're welcome."

He squeezed me, and then we settled into a gentle silence. His thumb brushed up and down on my forearm, where his hand rested. My arousal had tapered off to a very low buzz, and I felt comfortable.

"Do you work at Helping Hands tomorrow?" he asked.

"I'm going to swing by and help with some yard work in the afternoon, I think, but that's all."

His chest rose and fell beneath me, and I thought I could feel his heartbeat. But probably I was just being overly romantic.

"Would you come over here in the evening?"

"For more rope?"

"Perhaps. Perhaps other things."

"Other parts of the game?"

He chuckled, low in his throat. "I suppose you could call it that. Will you come?"

I grinned. "Perhaps."

# Chapter Eight

As promised, there'd been no sex that night. We stayed cuddled on the sofa for an hour or so, talking occasionally, until we both decided it was time for me to head home. He said he felt that I was okay to drive. I hadn't had but half a drink, so I agreed. I didn't commit to returning on Sunday, but I already knew in my head I was going to go. The things he did and the way he made me feel—that was rare. And I wanted more of it. More of him. I would try to figure out the hunter-prey thing another time. When my brain was working.

Sunday morning went by with me trying to concentrate on some work for Monday. I wasn't very effective. Then a shower and into Helping Hands for weeding the veggie garden. It was pretty uneventful. Jessie had gone to the Farmers Market, and Annette was festooning the dining room with some new table clothes and summer decorations someone had donated. When I walked in, she'd been hanging blinking lights shaped like chili peppers in the doorways. She was completely in her element.

I'd been in the dirt of the vegetable garden with another woman named Mirabella—a resident of the shelter—for about an hour when Annette came running outside.

"Caly! Are you out here?"

I ran my forearm over my head, wiping away sweat. "Right here. What's wrong?"

"Oh, nothing's wrong. You have a visitor, though!" She waved a hand toward the door. "Go on. He's in the office."

My heart beat at double time. Maybe it was Evan. I didn't know why he'd go into Annette's office, when he probably expected to see me tonight. My cheeks heated. Maybe he brought more rope. I stood and wiped my hands on my cargo shorts. I was really a mess.

"Would you hurry up, lazy bones?"

I cocked my head at her, and she laughed.

"Go!"

"I'm going!" I stalked into the building.

I made a pit stop at the public bathroom to at least wash my hands. While I sudsed up, I wondered why Evan wouldn't just come out back. I couldn't imagine anyone else showing up. Maybe Tessa, but she would have called first. I looked up, into the mirror. My hair was all over the place. Okay, short hair doesn't really have a lot of places to go, but I'd sweated and wiped my head over and over again. It looked worse than bedhead. And dirt streaked my face. Ugh.

I took yet another moment to wash my face, which essentially left me with a clean face and dirty everything else. I decided I'd be in that bathroom for an hour if I tried to get everything clean. I dried up with a paper towel, and then stepped out of the bathroom.

"Are you not in my office yet?" Annette was just coming in from the yard.

"God, woman, I had to get cleaned up. Who are you, my mother?"

"Pffft." She waved a hand at me and went off in the direction of the women's sleeping rooms.

When I got to her office, it wasn't Evan waiting for me. I wasn't sure if I winced, but I definitely felt an internal wince when Thomas turned around and smiled.

"Hey," he said.

"Hi." Guilt assailed me. I had never returned any of his phone calls. I'd been too busy with Evan. "I...I didn't expect you here."

"Tessa told me you were volunteering this weekend. I hope this is okay."

"Yes, of course." It really wasn't. What was I supposed to say to him? *"Listen, sorry that I haven't called you back. It's been a crazy week."* That would be lame.

"It's okay. I know you've got a lot going on and this is very short notice, but are you interested in getting dinner tonight? I mean, I'm sure you'll want to go home and clean up. Yard work is messy business." He gave me the sweetest look.

*Really, universe? This is what you're doing to me?*

"Um... Tonight isn't good. I'm sorry."

"Maybe tomorrow or Tuesday?"

I thought a moment. Where was this thing with Evan going? I mean, it wasn't like we were dating or anything. We hadn't even been out to a meal together except that disastrous lunch. And Thomas was a nice guy. "Yeah, tomorrow should be okay."

You'd have thought I'd handed him the winning lottery ticket. His entire face lit up, and his smile widened, if that could be believed. "Great! Pick you up at seven?"

"Let me meet you somewhere. I'm not sure how long I'm going to be at the office. I've got court in the morning, and then I have a couple briefs to write. I may have to come straight from work."

He nodded. "I totally understand. Do you have a restaurant preference?"

*Ugh.* Too many questions. "No. Anywhere is fine. You pick and let me know."

His smile didn't falter; in fact it seemed to get wider yet. It was a good smile—even and genuine. But there were no dimples. "So, I need to get back."

"Oh, right! Yes. Thanks for taking the time to see me." He bent toward me, hesitated, pulled back a little, then leaned in and planted a small kiss on my cheek. When he pulled away again, his entire face had gone red.

Well, that was sort of charming in a socially awkward way. "I'll see you tomorrow night, then," I said as I motioned toward the door with a sweep of my arm.

"Yes. Thanks." He moved past me and out into the main room. I followed. "Tomorrow," he said.

I waved to him as I headed toward the back door. "See you then."

—➤➤◄◄◄—

The weeding wasn't quite finished when I had to go, but Mirabella was still there, and two of the men had come out to help as well, so I wasn't worried about it getting done. I rushed home—yes, rushed. I was annoyed at myself for how much I was looking forward to whatever Evan had planned for tonight.

Shower, shave, makeup, hair, clothes. Matching lace bra-and-panty set this time. Condoms in my purse. We'd talked during the day and planned to meet before dinnertime, at five, so I thought we might either get or make something to eat, but I nibbled on some fruit and cheese before I went, just in case. Protein bar in my purse too.

The ride over was uneventful. So much so that I didn't really remember it. I was on autopilot. Half the time, I wondered and speculated about what was about to happen. The other half, I relived the night before, complete with shivers and squirming in my seat. By the time I got to his driveway, I was about ready to pounce him at the entryway.

When he answered the door, my readiness to pounce did not go away. He wore fitted khakis and a brick-red polo shirt that spanned his chest well, defining his muscles. His expression was of open welcome as he moved aside to let me in.

"I'm glad you came," he said as he closed the door. The *snick* of the lock catching made my stomach drop and my nerves tingle. "How was the gardening?"

"Dirty, mostly. But we got a lot done, so it was worthwhile."

"Good." He took my purse from me and set it on the table beside a black sash lying there. "Will you turn around, please?" He lifted the sash and watched me.

"Excuse me?"

"I would like to put a blindfold on you. Will you turn around?" His eyes twinkled.

A shiver went down my spine. But I turned my back to him. The blindfold came down over my eyes, and I closed them. He tied the scarf behind my head. I touched the fabric, felt the pressure of my fingers through the cool threads.

Evan's warm hands pressed against my upper arms, and he turned me around. The darkness surrounded me, but I felt his warmth and his breath against my neck as he whispered in my ear. "Do you trust me?"

How did he do that? Make my whole body a live wire? Make every inch of my skin wake up? "Yes, I trust you." And I did.

"Good." He turned me around again and moved behind me. He steered me forward with his hands on my upper arms again. My low-heeled shoes tap-tapped through the living room. The sound was muffled as I crossed a corner of the Oriental rug, then began on the hardwood again as we passed to the other side of the living room.

The air around me felt smaller. The hallway? We went a few paces, and then he turned me to the right. I stepped onto carpet, and the spicy smell of cloves filled my senses. However long this thing lasted with Evan, cloves would forever remind me of him. Soft classical music played as he directed me forward, then turned me around and backed me up. My calves bumped into a piece of furniture, and Evan placed his hands on top of my shoulders and then gave gentle pressure.

"Sit, please," he said in a soft voice.

I sat. I sank into what I guessed was an overstuffed chair or sofa. I ran my hands along the fabric on either side of my thighs. Soft, like velvet.

Evan had crouched at my feet. I found I was acutely aware of his heat in relation to me. I could feel his body when he moved around mine. He lifted one of my feet, his palms warm on my ankle. Electric sparks shot up my leg, straight to my pussy, my nipples—hell, to the tips of my fingers.

"You wore a very nice outfit tonight." He slid the pump off my foot, then switched and did the same to the other.

"Thank you."

"But I would like to take it off. I will leave your bra and panties on if you wish."

I couldn't tell if he was asking permission or just letting me know what he was going to do. That was answered when he took my hands and stood me up. He remained close enough for me to breathe his scent—that strange sweetness along with the cloves.

They say that when you lose one sense, others are heightened. That seemed to be the case. Each time his fingers brushed my skin as he unbuttoned my blouse, little shocks ran through me and goose bumps rose.

He seemed to move slowly, with deliberation. The first button. The second. The third. Until he'd gone all the way down to my waist. Then he pushed the shirt back, over my shoulders and partially down my arms. His palms skimmed along my exposed skin. When he stopped, I realized that he'd pinned my arms with my own blouse.

Heat gathered deep in my belly as he moved those palms along my chest and down my torso with a featherlight touch. I felt his body move and then his breath on my tummy. His hands crept lower to the waist of my skirt.

I shivered. I couldn't help it. And then his soft lips brushed the skin just above my belly button. I sucked in a breath as my insides melted. He made a soft, growly noise as he unfastened the hook. He drew the zipper down so slowly I fancied that I heard every tooth. Then he slid the skirt down my hips, and it whooshed into a pile at my feet.

Now he took a deep breath, and my skin flushed hot as the thought crossed my mind that he might smell me. I was suddenly shy. Embarrassed. I'd never, as an adult woman, felt that way around a man. Not if there was going to be sex. I didn't even know whether there was going to be sex.

Evan stood, his body very close to mine as he rose. So close that his shirt scraped against my breasts. My nipples, already hard inside my bra, ached at the touch. I tried not to moan. He slid my blouse the rest of the way off my shoulders, and it fell to the ground with a soft rustle.

He took my hands again and said, "Step out of your skirt, please."

I did so, following his lead on my hands. The carpet cushioned my soles, soft and textured, cool against my feet. He continued to move, and I went with him for several paces. Finally he stopped and laid my hands on what felt like cool, smooth upholstery. Leather, perhaps.

"I want you to feel the surface of this so that you will understand how to get onto it."

Apprehension tickled at the back of my mind. How many different ways are there to get onto a piece of furniture? I ran my hands over the smooth leather. It felt like a bench, but a bit too high and narrow to sit on and angled a little higher on one end than the other. There was no back. Evan moved one of my hands to the side and a bit lower where there was another padded bench-like surface that ran the same length and was angled the same but was even narrower — it wouldn't be comfortable to sit on. He walked me to the other side, and I felt another of the narrower parts. It must have been identical to the first.

He moved me again, this time stopping me at what I thought must be the foot of the thing. I realized the wider bench was in the middle with the narrower ones to the sides, something like a picnic table, but obviously smaller. They were all leather and padded. I felt Evan tap one knee and then guide my hand to the lower bench on that side.

"Knees go here." Then he took my hand and placed it on the wider, middle bench. "Body goes here. Do you understand?"

"Yes." Apparently I was supposed to straddle it like a horse and then lie forward. This was just weird. It wasn't until I'd climbed on top—carefully, because I was blind— that I realized what a vulnerable position I was in. My knees rested on the narrow padded beams on either side, as did my elbows—now I understood the reason for the angle. And that meant that my legs were spread, the front of my pussy pushed right against the padded middle bench while the rest... Well, if I hadn't had panties on, there would have been *nothing* left to imagination.

"Are you comfortable?" Evan ran his hand up my back, caressing my skin.

"This is weird."

"You've never been on something like this."

"Well, no." His statement struck me as dumb. Of course I'd never been on anything like this. Who had this sort of thing in their house? "What are you going to do?"

"Play the game a little bit."

"What does that mean?" Anxiety rode my spine. I second-guessed whether I really wanted to be here. I did want to spend time with Evan. But did I want whatever he had planned to do to me? I didn't know.

"Mostly pleasure. Maybe a little bit of pain—"

I lifted myself up on my hands and pushed so I was sitting up in a straddle on the strange bench. I reached for the blindfold, but his hand caught mine. I felt him close again and then a caress on my jaw.

"If you wish to stop, you only have to say, 'Evan, stop,' and I will. You said when you arrived that you trust me. Do you still?"

I thought about it. Hard. What did he mean by pain? Did he mean he was going to punch me? Did he mean he was going to give me a little spanking? I didn't understand what he planned to do. But did I trust him? I didn't like not being in control. And I thought that was what was making me want to get up more than any fear of something he might do to me. He said he would stop immediately if I said to. And I believed him.

"Yes. I still trust you."

"Then you will lie back down."

I took a second to center myself and then eased forward again. I rested my torso on the wide bench, my arms on the side beams. Evan's hand lay on the back of my head, and his lips grazed my ear.

"Good girl," he whispered.

Why did those words make my pussy clench? I decided not to think about it. I'd unpack that shit later. Right now, my body was ready, and my mind was curious, if also a little apprehensive.

Evan's hands rested on my back, lightly at first. After a moment, he put a bit of pressure on, pushing down against me. He continued the compression until it felt as if he were trying to push the air from my lungs. I grunted, and the pressure eased. He ran his hands up to my shoulders and then down along my ribs right around to the rise of my ass. I'd worn red lace panties—and matching bra!—and the material was thin enough that the heat from his palms warmed my backside as they roamed.

"You are beautiful," he said in not quite a whisper, and I flushed. His hands continued their movements, coming around my ass cheeks to that sensitive spot where my thighs began. His fingertips along the skin there made my whole body shudder and little waves ran through me. I bit my lip, and the little stab of pain from my teeth kept me from moaning.

He tickled down my thighs, to the backs of my knees, but then his fingers went away. I took in a breath and felt my muscles loosen. I'd been completely on edge, tensed up, the entire time he'd touched me.

Noise came from my right, a muted rustling. A sound of fabric or something slipping over something else. Skin? I lifted my head, hoping to hear more closely, but the sound stopped. And then Evan was beside me again. His scent was in my head all the time now, so I could only tell by sound and by the feeling of his body heat near me.

Something soft and...furry? touched my back. It slid along my skin from the middle of my back, along my spine, up over one shoulder—a full shudder slid through me then—down my arm, and finally up again and across to the other side. It tickled, but in a continuous way so that the tickle wasn't the sort to make me laugh, but rather the sort that made my skin sensitive. The gentle touch soothed me, and I finally really relaxed. I didn't know how long it lasted, but I was pretty blissed-out by the time we had skin-to-skin contact again.

Evan's hands followed a similar path as the fur, but his touch was stronger, less gentle. When he got to my ass, he squeezed a cheek in each hand, his touch firm and then hard. His fingers dug into my flesh, causing little frissons of pain to skitter under my skin. I groaned. He squeezed again. And the entire time my pussy flooded. I tried not to grind down against the bench below me.

His touch slowly traveled down the outsides of my thighs, pausing to squeeze every once in a while. Then he moved to the inner thighs. Now his touch was featherlight, barely a tickle. My skin, tight and sensitive, tingled everywhere his fingers roamed. He began behind my knees and then moved on to the inner thighs. He inched his fingers up slowly…too slowly, zigzagging at a maddening pace.

When he finally reached the apex, where my panty-covered pussy waited, I held my breath. I willed him to touch me. Willed him to do anything to give me contact. I wanted to hump the bench.

He ran a finger on each side of my pussy, where my thighs met it, just where the edges of my panties lay. His fingertips traced the panties there, from front to back. He left electric sparks in his wake and a shiver along my spine. When his touch disappeared, I released my breath in a long mewling groan.

Behind me, he chuckled. "We will get there."

I pressed my forehead against the leather and filled my lungs again. Everything was heightened, all my nerves exposed. Evan moved to my left side and put an arm across my back at my waist. His other hand rubbed a big circle around my ass.

"I am going to warm your backside a little bit. Will you stay still?"

I'd never been spanked as a child. My parents were hippies—hence my name, Calypso. So they'd never raised a hand to me. I'd never been struck in my life. I had no idea if I *could* stay still. "I'll try."

"Good."

I waited for the "girl" but it never came. A part of me wilted a little bit. His hand disappeared from my ass and then came down on it with a *thwap!* A jolt shot through me from the impact, and I jumped. Warmth spread over my body. He hadn't hit hard... Well, not so hard that I was ready to stop. He rubbed the spot he hit, and the contact soothed me. Then his hand moved to the other cheek. When he drew his hand away, I tensed, waiting.

And waiting.

He rubbed the small of my back with his other hand, and I relaxed. And then *smack!* Heat fanned out across my ass, and I about flew up off the bench.

"Ow! Goddammit!"

He pressed his palm between my shoulder blades. "Down."

I dropped back into position, grumbling under my breath. "That fucking hurt," I said to him.

"Yes."

I wanted to smack him.

So why did I stay on that bench? Why didn't I just get up?

He rubbed across my ass again, gently, pausing here and there to massage and knead. Then his hand came away, and he hit me again, not as hard as his second hit, but still hard enough for discomfort. He fell into an easy rhythm and intensity, not hitting harder or softer, moving around his target, never hitting the same spot twice in a row.

The pain melded all together with the rhythm and shifted from sharp to a muted, even feeling of heat on my skin, under my skin. I squirmed on the bench and made little sounds with each hit. I realized my breath came in heavy pants. As he kept on with the spanking, everything in my lower half felt hot. Some from the spanking, some from the growing arousal gathering in me. As I squirmed, my mound rubbed against the bench's leather padding. It sent little waves through me. I moaned.

He stopped and rested his hand on one ass cheek. His palm, warm before, now felt hot as a stove eye against my own burning skin. I struggled to catch my breath.

His other hand, the one that had been on the small of my back, holding me in place, moved to the other cheek. The coolness felt amazing, and as he rubbed little circles over my abused flesh, I realized I was grinding into the bench. Heat flooded my face.

His fingers tickled over the fabric covering my pussy. Hot, heavy pulses shot through me. I groaned again and leaned back into his hand, but he moved it just enough to keep the same pressure. That was to say, very little pressure. Not enough pressure. I slid back just a hair, hoping to get more contact.

He patted my butt and said, "Stay." And then he stepped away from me.

I laid my head to the side, cheek against the now warm leather, and let out a sigh. If we'd been playing my game, I'd have just told him I was ready to get off and then directed him how to do it. But obviously that wasn't going to work here.

Something small but hard pressed against my pussy. Not his finger, but at this point, I'd take what I could get.

I felt him wedge whatever it was between my slit and the bench. It pressed right against my clit. Then he was back at his place beside me, one hand on my back and the other on my ass. I'd thought we were done with the spanking part. But apparently I was wrong.

He started again, and this time it felt harder, sharper. I didn't know if it hurt a little more because I was already sore or because he was actually hitting me with more force. Each strike brought pain, heat, pressure. And each one pushed me against the thing under me, rubbing my clit, sending little frissons of electricity skittering through me.

The pain and the pleasure mixed and everything became bigger. Became hotter. Became more.

He paused for a moment in the spanking, rubbed my ass, and then fiddled with the thing under me. It suddenly sprang to life with a soft buzz. A vibrator! I shifted to the right and left just a little, and it rubbed my clit back and forth. I rode the heat, rode the wave as it got bigger.

Smack!

"Ahh!" I hadn't expected… I'd thought we were done. Again. But Evan began spanking me much harder, forcing my pussy tight against the vibrator with each stroke.

I lost track of the pain. I lost track of the pleasure. Every nerve in me was a live wire. I braced my hands on the lower beams, and it didn't even matter what I looked like anymore. I ground myself against that vibrator. I angled my hips up and down, meeting his hand for each smack. I heard each breath punctuated by a high-pitched moan, but it was like I was hearing someone else. In the blackness behind my eyes, fireworks exploded.

I let out a sharp cry, and he didn't stop.

He didn't stop.

The wave of my orgasm crashed over me, graying out the world. The only thing I knew was that crest, that intense, alive feeling as it took my body and my mind.

I only barely registered Evan slowing down, becoming more gentle as the orgasm leveled and the tide went out. I collapsed on the bench, angling my pussy away from the vibe. Too sensitive. My pulse beat in every cell.

Evan rubbed my ass with one hand, and I felt the vibrator taken away. All I could do was heave in breath after breath.

After a moment, both his hands rubbed over my ass, one on each cheek. Then he moved up, drawing large circles across my back, then shoulders. I was like jelly already, but the touch felt so good. I mewled my appreciation.

I wasn't sure how long I lay there. I didn't care much about time. Eventually I became aware of Evan closer to my head, his hands ministering my shoulders and neck. I cracked open one eye and came face-to-face with his erection. The blindfold had slid down my nose, giving me a view just above the fabric. His cock tented his boxer briefs, just like last night.

I reached out and brushed my fingertips against the straining fabric, his cock beneath it. The heat and the solidity of it made me want it in my mouth.

He shifted his hips and took a step to the side, taking his cock away. I reached farther.

"No," he said.

I froze. "Why not? I want to make you feel good too."

"I already feel good. We will have time enough for that later."

Why didn't he want me? I was good enough to tie, good enough to spank, but not good enough to fuck? To even give him a blowjob, for fuck's sake? This was twice in a row. What was wrong with me?

I pushed myself up without warning him, and he stepped back. I yanked the scarf off my head, and the dim light in the room blinded me for a moment. I blinked against it.

"What's wrong?"

"Why are you doing this?"

His brow furrowed, and he gave a slight shake of his head.

"This!" I waved my arm around the room—which was decorated very strangely, now that I had a chance to see it. Sort of like a medieval dungeon, but without the dripping walls. "Not this, like here, but this, like this!" I pointed to the bench and then my ass.

He rested a hand on my thigh and gave me one of those nice smiles. "It's part of the game."

I wasn't sure whether I wanted to be part of the game anymore. I hiked myself off the bench and went to my clothes, arranged in a neat pile on a brown, microfiber couch. I was stepping into my skirt when Evan came beside me.

"Caly." He put a hand on my back. "Stop, please."

I pulled the skirt the rest of the way up, fastened it, and then stopped moving. I didn't look at him. I suspected I was acting irrationally, but I didn't want to look too closely at it. I didn't know exactly why I was upset. I just was.

"Look at me please."

I wrinkled my nose and then moved my gaze up to his.

"Can we talk?"

I sighed heavily and grabbed my shirt. Since when did guys want to talk about all the things? Couldn't I just storm out and be done with it? I shrugged into the blouse and buttoned up. When I looked at him again, he had a hand held out, motioning to the couch. I dropped down with a huff.

Evan sat beside me, angled a little so that we were face-to-face. "Will you tell me what's going on?"

I paused. I didn't even know what was going on. How could I tell him? "I don't know."

"Okay. Then what are you feeling?"

Great. Out of all the guys in the city, I had to get the touchy-feely one. "I'm angry. I'm upset. I don't know why."

"All right. That's a start at least. Was there anything that happened that you wish hadn't?"

I thought on that. Was there? Not really crazy about the whole pain thing, but if I was honest with myself, that was a fucking phenomenal orgasm. So I didn't have any real problems with the pain. Obviously not with the vibrator. I had actually been feeling really good. I thought about where the good ended and the anger began. "Why won't you let me touch you?" I wanted to look at him full in the face, but I felt vulnerable. More vulnerable even than I'd felt on the bench, exposed.

He rested his fingertips on the edge of my leg. "Because this wasn't about me. This was about you."

When I finally brought my gaze up, his expression was frank and earnest.

"When I said there would be time enough for me later, I was being honest. There will be."

"I think I need to go."

He studied my face for a long moment and when I couldn't deal with it anymore, I stood. He rose too. "All right," he said. "If you're sure."

I slid my heels on before I replied. "I'm not sure of anything. That's part of the problem. And I can't figure any of it out here." I wanted to thank him, because that's my inclination when I've spent time with someone. But what would I thank him for? *Hey, thanks for the beating and the orgasm?* It was better just to skip it.

I went to the kitchen. The clock read 6:07. It had barely been an hour.

# Chapter Nine

I thought about calling out of work Monday morning but then decided I'd make myself crazy if I stayed home. So I went into the office and mostly puttered through the day mindlessly. Luckily for me—and my clients—I didn't have anything serious in court. Two continuances, and then the rest of the day at the office.

I spent most of the time thinking about the night before. I alternated between being horny and being annoyed at myself for overreacting. Because that's what I decided I'd done. Completely overreacted. The crappy thing was that I actually liked Evan. I wanted to spend more time with him. Now I was embarrassed to even talk to him. He must have thought I was an idiot. Or crazypants.

Just before lunch, I got a text from Thomas. I'd completely forgotten about dinner with him tonight. But he hadn't. He texted me the restaurant—a small French place— and let me know he was looking forward to spending time with me.

*Ugh.* I didn't feel like I was in a frame of mind to go out. But I'd blown off his calls all last week, so I'd feel really shitty blowing off our first date too. And who knew? Maybe he was my perfect Prince Charming. Maybe we'd go on this date and I'd be in love by the main course.

I was skeptical, but I supposed stranger things had happened in life.

Once I'd dealt with his texts, my mind went immediately back to Evan. If I thought about it, I could still feel the heat of his cock beneath my fingers, how it warmed the stretched fabric of his boxer briefs. I shook my head to clear it. I had opinion reports to review. I didn't need to be spending all this time thinking about Evan and his damned cock that he wouldn't even let me fucking see.

I ordered lunch and ate at my desk. My paralegal was in and out, checking on me. She had a keen feeling for when I was off my game. And, really, I'd been off my game for a while now, hadn't I?

My phone buzzed. I didn't want to deal with Thomas anymore. I thought about ignoring it, but considered that I hadn't heard from Tessa yet, so it could have been her.

*Evan: I'm checking on you. How are you feeling?*

I stared at the screen. I tried not to feel elated that Evan was thinking of me. It didn't work very well. I *was* elated that he was thinking of me.

*Me: I'm okay. Working.*

Not working very efficiently, but I was *at* work. That counted.

*Evan: You might feel overly emotional sometime in the next couple days. Could start today or tomorrow or even the next day. That's normal.*

What the hell was that supposed to mean? It's not like I wasn't already fucking overly emotional. Was he being snarky?

*Me: Yeah, thanks.*

*Evan: Will you call me if you need to talk?*

Would I? I didn't know. I was still embarrassed by my storming out. But he didn't seem to be. I had no idea how he couldn't think I was unhinged. But there he was, texting me.

*Me: Yes, okay.*

*Evan: Good. And I'm serious. You will likely need some attention from me.*

Okay, now he was just being narcissistic. I didn't need him. Even if I was emotional and even if I did like him, that didn't mean I needed him. Hell, I'm a woman. I deal with excessive emotion every damn month.

*Me: Whatever you say.*

*Evan: Just don't be afraid to reach out.*

*Me: I'm not afraid.*

*Evan: Good.*

Even over text, he made me want to smack him. *Sheesh.*

I put the phone away and went back to the decision reports. For whatever reason, I was actually able to concentrate for a little while. I got involved, and before I realized it, my paralegal stuck her head in to let me know she was heading home. It was almost six already.

Time to go make myself pretty for Thomas.

⟶⟫⟪⟵

I was glad we'd agreed to arrive separately, because I spent the whole drive to the restaurant thinking about how unexcited I was.

I'd decided on a simple sundress that fell just past my knees, along with a light cardigan. The dress gave me great cleavage—which is, of course, important. A pair of wedge sandals, seashell earrings with a matching necklace, and I was set.

When I arrived, he was sitting at the tiny bar in the corner of the bistro. He'd dressed up way more than I did, in his suit and tie. I had a sinking feeling in my stomach that this wasn't going to go well.

He caught my eye, and his entire face lit up with a smile. I couldn't help comparing his reaction to Evan's, when he smiled with his whole face. Thomas was perfectly fine. But I suddenly realized that I liked Evan's dimple better.

I gave my head a little shake, hoping to dislodge Evan from my mind. Thomas's expression faltered a little, and I hurried over to him, fixing my own smile on my face. "I'm not late, am I?"

"No, no. I've only been here a few minutes." He motioned to his microbrew that didn't even looked sipped at. "Would you like a drink?"

"Maybe when we sit down."

"All right. Let's get our table."

Once we were settled in and had ordered drinks— amaretto for me, his beer still for him—he started with the small talk. This was the stuff I had never been good at. Hunting didn't really require it.

"You said you do work at Helping Hands, right? With Annette and Jessie."

"Yes," I said. "I spend a lot of my time there, actually. Most of my weekends are taken up with volunteering."

"How is the new building going?"

"Well, I'm not really too involved with that part. I'm only included because I'm the one who brought Helping Hands to the partners' attention."

"Really? That's amazing. You're the reason everything happened, then. Your firm never would have had that fund-raiser if you hadn't gotten it in front of them."

"Perhaps not." I stared into my drink. This was really uncomfortable.

"I mean, they're getting a brand-new building. Jessie told me last week that because of all the publicity, several of the furniture stores have offered to donate beds and kitchen tables." He'd leaned forward in his seat with his enthusiasm.

"Yes, that is good news." I chugged a big mouthful of the amaretto. It warmed my throat as it went down. I wondered what Evan was doing tonight. Then I chided myself.

"And I suspect that's not going to be the last of the offers either. There's so much good press to be had. Companies are going to be lining up to help."

"I hope so."

"And all because you focused your firm's attention on that one small shelter."

I knew he was beaming at me, but there was no way I was going to look at him. Subject change. "You're a therapist, right? You have your own practice?"

"I do, though I split my time between it and the hospital's addiction floor."

*Thank God.* A new line of conversation. "Have you always done rehab counseling?"

"No. Right out of school, I did a lot of couples counseling and just general counseling. I found I really enjoyed helping folks who struggle with addiction. It can be such a difficult path. If I can make it even a little bit easier, then it's worthwhile."

The server came, but we hadn't even looked at the menus. She gave us another minute, and that gave us an opportunity to not talk. I couldn't help thinking that conversation with Evan was a lot easier. Then I had to admit to myself that conversation with Evan is also a lot more frustrating. But at least it was interesting.

Although, if I were honest, we didn't really have much in the way of conversation. And, if I were *really* honest, I'd admit that most of our conversations had ended in fighting. Hmmm.

I ordered a salad with lots of weird things on it. Thomas ordered escargot and some other item I didn't recognize. I didn't mind snails, but I wasn't a huge fan.

"So did you always want to be a lawyer?" he asked.

God, this was going to be a long night.

-→➤◄-

He walked me to my car. I tried to tell him that I was fine, but he wasn't taking any sort of hints. So much for being in love by the main course. I hadn't even wanted to stay for dessert.

"So," he said as I pointed out my gray sedan and we moved in that direction, "maybe Mexican for our second date?"

Prior to this whole thing with Evan that had caused me to forget how to deal with men, I knew how to handle situations like this. It was a lot like my guys wanting to stay the night, which was not something that happened. Ever. This wasn't really all that different. This was just kicking him out before he ever got to the bed. I'd done this dozens of times.

I stopped at my car door, turned, and faced him. "Thomas. I had a nice time, but I don't really think we're compatible."

Crestfallen. That was the only way to describe the look on his face. "But…"

"I think we'd make good friends. But that's really all." It wasn't always easy being this honest, but it saved a lot of hassle in the end. Plus, it hurt less to be rejected at the beginning than after some time has gone by.

"Was it really that awful?" Ice in his voice. Not angry ice, but defensive ice. The sort of ice wall that someone built to freeze another person out. That was good. It would help him.

"I just said it wasn't awful."

"But you don't want to see me again."

Okay, willful ignorance annoys me. "When did I say that?"

"You just said you didn't think we are compatible."

"Yes. That doesn't mean you're dead to me. It just means that I don't think we'd work out romantically."

"Why not?"

*Good God. Petulance is so not sexy.* "I don't have to list any reasons. I just don't feel like we'd work out that way." I hit the Unlock button on my key fob, and my car made the comforting double beep that invited me to come sit inside. That was exactly where I wanted to be.

"I'd really like a reason." He stood stiffly and spoke as if he had a right to order me around.

Little warnings went off in the back of my head. Suddenly, the parking lot seemed a lot darker than it had originally. "I'm sorry. I don't have one to give you beyond what I've already said." I pulled open the car door as he stepped toward me. "Thomas." My lawyer voice. The one that commanded attention in the courtroom. He stopped. "I'm going home now."

He sighed, and the air of danger dissipated. "I just wish you'd give me a chance."

I did, I thought. But I decided I wasn't going to say that. "Good night, Thomas."

The relief I felt once I'd slid into the driver's seat and closed the door surprised me. I didn't realize how tense I had been. He stepped away from the car as I started the engine. I didn't look directly at him, just pulled away.

# Chapter Ten

I wasn't three miles from the restaurant and my hands shook so hard I decided to pull over, afraid I was going to wreck the car. My heart pounded like it was trying to escape from my body. My breathing had gotten shallow, and little flashes began around the edges of my vision. I concentrated on taking normal breaths just so I wouldn't pass out. I had no idea why I was freaking out more now that I was away from Thomas than I had been when I was with him.

I suddenly remembered Evan's text about being emotional. I wondered if this was what he meant. He'd said to call him, but how douchey would it be to call a guy after having had a date with a different guy? That was just dumb.

I took a long, deep breath and turned on my music. That would help, I was sure. My shaking had already eased up. I tried not to think about the tone of Thomas's voice as he demanded I give him a reason why I didn't want to see him. But like anything else, just concentrating on trying not to think about it made me think about it. And again with the shaking.

I was just freaking myself out. And each time I did, I went back to Evan's texts. I pulled out my phone and opened them up. Maybe rereading would make me stop thinking about them.

*Evan: Will you call me if you need to talk?*

I'd thought that was a dumb thing…that I wouldn't possibly need to talk to him. But maybe I did. Maybe that was exactly what I needed.

I checked the time. Barely past eight thirty. There went the easy excuse for not calling—being too late. It wasn't too late.

I pulled him up on the contact list and closed my eyes for a moment. I tried to decide whether I really wanted to do this.

And I couldn't decide. I kept going back and forth, back and forth. Finally, I opened my eyes, took a breath, and punched Talk. It was better to just do it. The thinking wasn't helping at all.

He picked up on the second ring. "Hello."

I didn't speak for a second and then realized it seemed like a dramatic schoolgirl thing to do. "Evan. It's Caly. You said to call."

"I did. Are you all right?"

"I… I'm not really sure why I'm calling you. It seems weird."

"All right." He wasn't short with me. Patience came through in his tone. "What's happening?"

"I… Um. I actually pulled over to the side of the road because I was afraid I might get into an accident."

Silence for a moment, and then he said, "Okay. Have you been drinking?"

"Well, I had one drink with dinner, but that isn't why. I freaked out a little bit. I was out to dinner with someone and he... Well, it just didn't end well."

"Did he hurt you?" The tightness in his voice made me wince. But it also made my belly wobble.

"No, no. Nothing like that." Because I got away, said a small voice in my head. "I'm fine. Just a little shaken up."

"Would you like to come here?"

Yes, I realized. That was exactly what I wanted. Exactly. "Is that okay? I wouldn't be interrupting anything, would I?"

"I don't invite people over if I don't want them over, Caly." I could hear the shift to a smile. "You shouldn't ever worry about that."

My cheeks heated. Why the hell was I blushing? "Then yes, I would like to come over."

"Are you okay to drive?"

I noticed that my hands were no longer shaking. My heart wasn't racing, and my breathing was even and level. "Yes. I think I've calmed down enough."

"Good. Where are you?"

"I'm about fifteen minutes from you."

"All right. I will expect you then. Be careful. And if you feel you can't make it, call me. I will come and pick you up. Do you understand?"

"Yes." My whole body felt warm.

"Good. I'll see you soon."

As I pulled into his driveway, the side door opened and he stepped out. Jeans and a polo shirt. I was now beginning to suspect suits were not his wardrobe of choice, contrary to all our early interactions. I released a breath as soon as I saw him, and relief flooded me. I decided not to try to unpack that. I was just glad to no longer feel anxious. Then I realized that I was doing a lot of not-unpacking when it came to Evan.

I grabbed my purse and got out of the car. By the time I'd turned to close my door, he was there. When I faced him, he put his hands on my upper arms and stared at me.

"You're all right?"

"Yes." I nodded to punctuate my answer.

"Come in." He guided me into the house and closed and locked the kitchen door behind him. A kettle whistled on the stove, and he turned the burner off. "I was just making some tea. Would you like a cup?"

I couldn't think of anything more perfect right at that moment. I wasn't much of a tea drinker, but that was...perfect. "Yes, please. With sugar and some milk?"

He half smiled at me. I couldn't tell if it was amusement in his eyes or appreciation. "Go on into the living room, and I'll bring it out in a minute."

I nodded and went, purse clutched against me. I thought I should feel nervous, but I really didn't. I considered the other two times I'd come into this room. I'd been very nervous then. Not so much now. Strange.

I settled onto the same place on the sofa I'd sat previously. Sort of my place. That thought made me happy.

I wasn't on my own long before he came in with two thick ceramic mugs, one dark red and the other a deep blue. "Color preference?"

"Um... Red."

He handed the mug to me. "Imagine my surprise when I learned that we take our tea the same way."

I laughed. I couldn't help it. What were the odds, really? He gave me that smile again as he sat beside me—his place on the sofa.

I blew on the steamy surface of the tea. The scent relaxed me even more. I took a small sip, but it was still just a titch too hot.

"Do you want to tell me what happened tonight?"

I didn't know whether I did or not, but I figured I at least owed him some explanation of why I suddenly invaded his Monday evening at home. I gave him a very short version of the conversation in the parking lot. He remained impassive as I spoke.

"I'm glad you left when you did," he said when I'd finished.

"Me too. I got a bad vibe from him just then."

"And you pulled over because you were having trouble focusing on driving?"

"Sort of." I took a swallow of my tea, and it warmed me in a way the amaretto hadn't. "I just felt shaky. Wobbly. I didn't want to chance driving in that condition, so I pulled over. That's when I called you."

"Thank you. I wasn't sure whether you would call if you needed me."

I waited a moment before I responded. I wasn't sure how transparent I wanted to be. But I felt safe, even though I also felt vulnerable. "I didn't know if this constituted need. And I wasn't sure you were serious about the offer either, after the way I acted last night."

He set his cup down, reached out, and laid a hand on my knee. It wasn't smarmy or weird. Just intent. "You can trust that I will never offer you something that I am not genuine about wishing you to have."

I clutched my own mug in both hands, letting the heat warm my palms. I felt such a mix of emotions right then that I couldn't pinpoint exactly what they were. "Okay."

"And don't worry about how you reacted last night. What you experienced was both very intense and also a very new thing for you. I don't doubt that you felt overwhelmed and lashed out for it. I was not offended."

I nodded, unable to say anything. It occurred to me that I felt forgiven. As if I'd gotten absolution for a sin.

He leaned back against the sofa and opened one arm to me. "Come here."

I placed my mug on the table beside his and curled into him. I slid my sandals off and drew my feet up beneath me. Once I'd settled, my head against his chest, my bent legs leaning against his thighs, he closed both his arms around me, encircling me in his warmth.

His chest rose and fell gently. The scent of him surrounded me, and I closed my eyes, content. He leaned his cheek against the top of my head, and his breath whooshed lightly through my hair. I'd felt more vulnerable here with him than I had in the parking lot with Thomas. But I also felt safer here. That dichotomy confused me. Safety and vulnerability never went hand in hand.

They never had in the past, anyway.

---

Evan woke me at some point. I must have dozed off.

"Caly, it's late. Let's get you into bed. I have a guest room you're welcome to stay in. Come on." He urged me to my feet. I was awake enough to realize I didn't want to sleep by myself.

"Do I have to?" We began moving through the room to the hallway.

"Yes. I don't want you driving home half-asleep."

"I mean do I have to sleep in the guest room?"

His step faltered for only a moment, but I felt it. "Where would you prefer to sleep?"

"I don't want to sleep alone."

"In my bed then?" His voice had dropped to a very low rumble that vibrated against my side, where he held me to him as we walked.

"Yes." I felt like I wanted to preface it, give conditions. But I was too tired. Or maybe I really didn't want to do those things. Maybe I just wanted to follow his lead. Go where he wanted to go.

"All right."

We went by what looked like a guest room and continued past a closed door—the room from last night?— through a doorway at the end of the hall. He turned on a dimmer, and the room filled with a dusty light.

A king-size bed dominated the room. It was low profile and sedate, with a dark wood base and a simple matching headboard. On the wall with the door we'd just entered through, a long dresser took the length, topped with a wide mirror. Two end tables flanked the bed on either side, and in the corner to the left was a door that probably led to a bathroom. Artwork hung on the walls in thin wooden frames, but I didn't want to spare enough attention to see what sort of art they were.

He led me to the bed. "Will you allow me to take off your dress?"

"Yes." Butterflies fluttered in my belly. The air filled with electric tension.

He slide the cardigan down my arms and off before laying it at the foot of the bed. He met my gaze, and his eyes smoldered as he hooked his fingers beneath the straps of my sundress. When they slipped free of my shoulders, he pushed the clingy material over my hips. The whole dress fell to the floor in a pool of fabric around my feet. I was reminded briefly of my skirt from last night.

He stilled and rested his hands very lightly on my shoulders. I watched him watching me and felt that strange mix of safe vulnerability again. He dipped his head, and his lips brushed against mine, lightly at first. Everything in me came alive. His right hand skimmed over my shoulder and to the side of my neck, warming my skin. I parted my lips just enough to peek my tongue out. I tasted tea on his lips before they opened and the tip of his tongue met mine.

My nipples hardened to little pebbles and lightning zinged through my entire body. I leaned into him, and his other arm wrapped around me. His clothes rubbed against the bare skin of my tummy, my thighs as he held me tight to him. His lips crushed mine, and his cock nudged against me.

Leaving me breathless, he broke the kiss. "I can't have you in my bed and not touch you."

I only nodded. He'd taken my words.

He released me, turned, and pulled the covers back. He looked at me and pointed to the bed. I crawled in, still wearing my bra and panties. For now, I guessed.

By the time I slid between the cool sheets and scooted back to leave him room, Evan had stripped down to his boxer briefs—gray today. I held the covers up, and he moved in beside me. The warmth of him and the scent of him overwhelmed me. I leaned onto the pillow and waited. It occurred to me that I was okay with this. I was okay with not taking the lead. It was an odd feeling—foreign. But with Evan, it seemed right.

He turned away for a second and reached for something on the nightstand. The lights dimmed, dark enough for sleep, but enough light to make things out. He rolled back to me and opened his left arm. I shimmied myself into the crook there and settled my head on his chest. His arm came to rest on mine, and his thumb brushed lightly over my skin.

"I am glad you came," he said.

"Me too." And that was true. Even lying here without doing all the sexy things—this felt comfortable. "But I am hoping for more kissing."

He looked down at me and I grinned. Then he barked out a laugh. "I think we can arrange more kissing." He shifted onto his side, cupped my cheek, and brought his lips to mine again. No tongue. Just a slow, sexy kiss with his fingers caressing my face and then slipping down toward my neck. Goose bumps rose all over, and I made a soft, mewling sound into the kiss. But he kept the pace slow and sensual.

Heat engulfed me, and I pressed against him. His hand slid down my shoulder and along my back. I waited for him to begin to unhook my bra, but he didn't. He just pressed his hand into me and held me fast. And kissed me.

Tingles went all the way to my toes. Kisses like this were rare, beautiful, and it got my juices going better than anything else could.

He pulled back, and I gasped a breath, my chest heaving. I wanted to rip his boxer briefs off and climb on top of him. But he just stared at me. After what felt like five minutes—but probably wasn't even one—it got uncomfortable for me. It was as if he was trying to see into me. I dropped my gaze. I knew I was blushing by the heat in my cheeks. I just hoped he couldn't see it in the dim light.

Evan brought his hand around and cupped my chin between his thumb and forefinger. He raised my head until my gaze met his. Then he smiled, just a small one, and crushed his lips against mine.

His tongue invaded my mouth, and I tasted tea again, but only faintly. His hand slid down my chin to my neck, pausing there for just a moment, his fingers wrapped around, firm against my skin. Then his hand was at my breast, and he squeezed it through the lace of my bra. I groaned and pivoted against him. His hard-on brushed my hip.

I lost all track of time as we made out. My lips against his, tongues raking alongside each other. I ran my hands along his chest, played with the hair there. I even reached behind and skimmed my fingers along his boxer-brief-covered ass. It was hard and tight.

His hands roamed just as much as mine did. He tweaked my nipples, which made me moan and squirm against him. It had been a long, long time since I'd been this turned on. His hand skated along my side, which is one of the most sensitive parts of my body, and I shivered. More goose bumps. He reached behind my thigh and hiked my leg up over his, then shifted onto his back, dragging me on top of him.

I really didn't care for this position at all. Yes, being fat hadn't stood in the way of me getting what I wanted, but this position always made me very aware of my size.

I lay on him, straddling his hips. His cock pressed against my pussy with two layers of fabric in between. I could still feel how hot and hard it was, though. I pushed my insecurities out of my mind just as he pulled me down to him and brought my lips to his. I ground my hips, forcing his cock up and down along my slit. On each down pivot, the head of his cock rubbed against my clit, sending electric shivers through me. Heat and tension gathered in my belly as we kissed. His growl reverberated in my mouth.

His hands ran up and down my back, along my sides. Every time his fingertips brushed that skin, I shuddered and ground down harder into him. My bra-covered breasts scraped along his chest, the lace keeping my nipples at peak.

We broke the kiss, both panting. I looked down at him. He stared at me, his eyes hooded and dark. I laid a kiss on the corner of his mouth, then another on his jaw. A soft sigh escaped his lips as I moved farther down: his neck, his collarbone, his chest. I paused at his left nipple long enough to tickle it with the tip of my tongue and then pull it into my mouth. It hardened up as I sucked on it gently. I flicked at his other nipple with my fingers.

I scattered a trail of kisses down his belly and paused just before his navel. I gazed up his body at his face. He watched me and then gave a little nod. I was glad he knew why I'd waited.

I continued my path down until my body was framed between his legs, and I held myself right over his still-covered cock. The sheets had slid off my back and puddled behind me, on top of his feet.

In the dim light, his cock strained mightily against the gray fabric, and I couldn't keep from running my fingertips over it. Firm, strong, and hot. I wrapped my hand around it over the boxer briefs and squeezed just a little. Evan growled low in his throat.

I released his cock and hooked my fingers under the waistband of his shorts. He lifted his hips and shifted so I was able to pull the offending garment off completely without moving from where I knelt. I deliberately didn't look at his cock until I'd tossed the underwear to the floor.

When I did swing my gaze back to him, I admired his cock for a long moment before I touched it again. It wasn't overly long, but it was thick and a little wider even at the base. The head was pronounced, with a heavy ridge, and the vein running along the top throbbed. His cock bobbed in the air.

I wrapped my fingers around it again, this time with no barrier between my skin and his. The dark head came up from my fist, looking strong and majestic. I'd never really thought of a cock as majestic before. I almost laughed at myself, but thought that would likely be misinterpreted.

I stroked up his cock and then down, slowly, watching his skin move over the firm muscle underneath. It occurred to me that he was uncut. When I sneaked a peek at his face, I found he had his head tilted back against the pillow and his eyes closed. His chest rose and fell with heavy breaths.

The hair around his cock and dusting his balls was trimmed neatly. I leaned down and pressed my face into the crook of his leg. His scent was spicier here, musky and masculine. I took a deep breath and squeezed his cock again. He gave a groan in response.

My pussy tingled, and I knew my panties were soaked. Normally, I'd move on to the fucking, but I was less concerned about my own pleasure right now, for some reason. I eyed Evan again, and his head was still tossed back, his lips parted slightly, as I rubbed the length of his cock.

I raised myself a bit and darted my tongue toward the head, looking for an experimental taste. I ran the flat of it along the underside of his head. He rewarded me with another deep groan. His hips bucked up, and his cock bumped my nose. I grinned. Socked in the nose with a cockhead.

*Enough messing around.*

I gave his cock another squeeze just as I wrapped my lips around the head. Out of the side of my eye, I saw his hand fist the sheets. His other hand moved to my shoulder, and his fingers brushed over my skin.

As I stroked, every time my hand moved down, I allowed my lips to follow, so his entire shaft was being touched either by my mouth or my fingers. I moved slowly, languidly, for a little while, letting his taste and his smell get into my senses. His thumb rubbed back and forth against my shoulder as I moved. And I began using my hand less and my mouth more. I'd been told I was good at giving blowjobs, but I really felt like it was just a matter of paying attention to the man's responses, learning his tells. For each moan I got from him, his thumb moved a little faster or pressed just a little harder. It let me gauge what I was doing.

Without warning, I drew my hand away and sucked him down to the root. His breath hitched. His entire body stiffened, and his hand stilled completely except to clutch at my shoulder. His cockhead nudged the back of my throat, and I concentrated on breathing through my nose so I wouldn't gag. That was the trick. Concentrating on something other than what was crammed down my throat.

When I felt like I was losing control of the gag reflex, I eased up his shaft, moving my tongue against his skin inside my mouth the whole time. He'd started making grunting sounds, and his thumb resumed rubbing the top of my shoulder. I held the base of his shaft tightly as I began to suck his cock, my head moving up and down over him.

I tilted just a bit so I could look up his body at him. He stared back, a hunger in his eyes. His hand shifted to my head, and he guided my movements. He didn't force me down, but gave me a little pressure when I came up so I'd know to move down faster. I moved with his indications, and he leaned his head back again.

"I'm close," he said. "When I say, change to just your hand."

I muffled an assent. He groaned again.

Now he raised his hips off the bed as I came down. His cockhead hit the back of my throat with each thrust, but we were both moving fast enough that it didn't trigger my gag. He battered the back of my throat.

I wanted him to come. I wanted it more than I wanted my own orgasm.

He gasped and pulled my head up by my hair. "Hand!"

I grabbed his cock and jerked up and down, fast. He wrapped his hand around mine and guided it, pumping his cock with me. He made a low rumble in his throat and arched his back. Cum shot from his cock in great spurts, landing on his belly, his chest, and the bed beside him.

He kept up the pace until the spurts became dribbles, and then he squeezed as he drew our hands up, the last bit of cum seeping out of the tip of his cock. He collapsed with a long sigh, a look of contentment settling over his features.

His hand still engulfed mine, wrapped around his cock, which had only softened a bit. "Mmmm. Excellent job." He peeked open an eye and peered at me. I laughed. He grinned as he opened both eyes and released his grip on my hand. Cum dribbled along his fingers and mine. He nodded toward the door in the corner. "Grab a washcloth from the bathroom, please."

I hopped up, careful not to touch anything with my messy hand, and made for the doorway. Inside the bathroom, I reached for the light switch with my clean hand and found — surprise — a dimmer switch, along with a couple other switches I wasn't sure about. I turned it on enough to see by. The bathroom was huge. It seemed out of place in this style of house, which, from the outside, looked like a typical middle-class family home.

Everything in the bathroom was marble or slate. The vanity had two sinks with elaborate faucets. In the corner was a giant Jacuzzi tub that could have easily fit four. The walls were actually rim-to-ceiling windows, which was probably gorgeous in the daytime, though I would wonder about nosy neighbors. In the other corner, but without windows, was an equally large shower with multiple heads on multiple walls and a marble bench along the far side. It was definitely not a single-person shower.

It took a moment for me to process how ridiculously lavish the bathroom was. I would have imagined something like this in a mansion or a summer home in the Hamptons (not that I'd ever been there).

I remembered my task, mainly because the cool air was causing the cum to dry on my hand, which was not the sexiest feeling ever. I went to one of the sinks and washed up. The warm water came very fast, and the soap smelled of cloves. I grabbed a washcloth from beneath the sink and wetted it. After squeezing out the excess, I went back into the bedroom.

Evan lay where I'd left him but propped up on more pillows with his clean hand behind his head. His eyes were closed, and he held his dirty hand up, his elbow on the bed.

I wrapped his hand in the washcloth. He didn't open his eyes, but he made happy sounds. "Mmmm. Warm." I cleaned his hand, then his chest and belly, then his cock. Lastly, I wiped the few drops from the bedsheets. I took the washcloth back to the bathroom and then returned to the bed. Evan patted the sheet on his left, meaning I'd have to crawl over him to get to the space. That wasn't really a hardship, though.

I deliberately rubbed my lace-covered breasts on his chest as I moved on top of him. I straddled him for long enough to press all my interesting parts into all his interesting parts. He watched me with an amused grin on his face.

"Enjoying yourself?"

"Not as much as you just did, but yes," I said as I flipped over sideways and landed on the bed. I stretched out, lying on my right side, and propped my head up on my hand. "This evening turned out better than expected."

He laughed. "Good. I'm glad. You deserve better than expected." He brushed his fingertip over my nose.

Everything in me warmed up. Not the sexy sort of warm—though there was still some of that too—but a different sort of warm that came from the idea that he valued me beyond sex.

That wasn't something that ever really played in my mind, usually. I mean, I know I have value beyond sex. I've never had an issue with self-worth or needing a man to validate me. But for some reason, hearing Evan say those words made me warm and fuzzy.

He reached back to the nightstand, and the lights lowered until the room was almost completely dark. "Lie down here." He wrapped his arm around me, and I settled against his chest again. In his free hand, he'd picked his phone up from the bedside table. He planted a kiss on the top of my head. "What time do you need to be up?"

"Are we done?"

"Yep."

I propped up on my elbow. "What about me?" I could barely see his outline in the darkness, let alone his expression.

"Well, feel free to take care of yourself if you'd like. But I recommend going to sleep."

Anger welled up in me so fast I could barely even grasp what he'd said. All the warm fuzzies disappeared. "Are you fucking kidding me?"

He didn't respond to my anger. He spoke with a level voice. "I don't believe in quid pro quo in the bedroom. Last night was your night. Tonight was mine. Another night soon will be for both of us. But not tonight." He paused, and I was at a loss for words. "Being as I don't have control over what you do, as I said, you're welcome to take care of yourself. If I had that control, however, you would be going to sleep." It sounded like he was smiling, but I couldn't tell whether it was snark or amusement.

"I didn't realize you were such a douche." Even with the words, though, I didn't get up from the bed.

"I don't think I am, but if you do, that's fine. I admit to finding it a little disappointing, but I will get over that."

And then it hit me. His game. This was all part of his game. Even though that felt true all the way to my bones, I didn't understand what the purpose was. Was he testing me for some reason? What was the point? Maybe he wanted to see how weak I was.

Because just letting him dictate my actions was definitely weak. *I think*. Everything was jumbled in my head. I'd gotten indignant with him before when he'd pushed my buttons. I'd even walked out on him. And he let me go. Would he now? Did I want to leave his bed? I couldn't tell if I was being taken advantage of or not.

"You have a beautiful mind, you know," he said.

"What?" Because apparently I wasn't already completely confused.

"I like that you are a thinker. You're a planner, yes, but more than that, you like to think. You try to work out all the obstacles and all the angles in your head. That's a rare trait."

I wasn't sure how to respond. *God!* I hated how he kept me just off my footing. *Argh!*

"I mention it," he continued, "because I know you're struggling right now. It's okay that you are. I'll wait until you decide what you wish to do. But if it means anything, I hope you will lie down with me and stay."

I didn't know whether he was trying to help my confusion or make it worse. I couldn't tell if he was trying to orchestrate something, trying to maneuver me into a corner. I hate men who do that more than anything. But I realized that I didn't hate Evan.

So what did I want to do? Besides understand what the fuck was going on, of course. Sleep would help clear my mind. But did I want to do that sleeping here, or in my own bed?

I thought about it. I didn't want to leave. Maybe Evan was trying to take advantage of me. Maybe he had some master plan, and I was walking right into it. I'd deal with that tomorrow. Right now, I wanted his arms around me.

I lay down against his chest once more, and his left arm wrapped me tight.

"What time do you need to be up?" He still had his phone in his hand.

"Seven, probably."

He programmed his alarm and then set the phone on the nightstand. He dropped another kiss on the top of my head, and I closed my eyes.

This would do for now.

# Chapter Eleven

When I woke up the next morning, the room was quiet. That fresh-shower smell was in the air. That one that says someone just got all sudsy clean. But the bathroom was dark. Evan wasn't anywhere to be seen.

I slid out of bed, still in my bra and panties. My dress lay in a heap on the floor, and my cardigan hadn't slipped from the foot of the bed. I pulled the sundress on over my head and grabbed the sweater. I padded down the hallway as I pushed my hands through the sleeves. Sounds came from the kitchen. A glance at the clock on the fireplace mantel showed six thirty. The scent of coffee hit my nostrils, and my stomach growled. Maybe he was making breakfast.

Sure enough, when I got into the kitchen, there was coffee waiting. Evan sat in one of the two bistro chairs at the high table in the room and sipped a cup while he read the newspaper.

"Good morning," he said with a wide grin. "There's fresh coffee. I left a mug out for you." He nodded to the counter. "Sugar's there beside the pot, and there's milk in the fridge if you like that."

So no bacon and eggs in bed. Ah well. I set about making my coffee—both cream and sugar—and then took the other chair. Evan folded his newspaper and set it down in front of him.

"How did you sleep?"

"Well, thanks. You?" This seemed awkward, but maybe it was just me. I wasn't used to waking up to someone.

"Like a log." He glanced around the kitchen. "Sorry. I'm not much of a breakfast person. I've got some bread. We can do toast if you'd like."

"No, I'm good. I don't eat right away anyway. Messes with my stomach." I took a sip of the steaming coffee. It was really, really good. Strong, with a nutty undertone. Evan definitely didn't skimp on the beans.

"Busy day today?"

"I have a couple meetings with clients, but mostly today is a research day. No court this week, but I've got a pretty important one on the docket next week."

He nodded. "Do you want to shower here or go home?"

Ahh. Here it was. The let-me-show-you-the-door phase. "I'll go home. I don't have a change of clothes here anyway." I took another swig of my coffee and slid off the seat, already resigned to leaving. "I think I left my purse in the living room. I'll just grab it real quick."

Evan's hand wrapped around my wrist. My gaze flew up to his.

"Stop for a moment, please."

I just stared at him. I felt like a deer in headlights.

"You don't have to go running off immediately. I was only asking your plans. That's all. Now take a breath." Humor danced in his eyes, and rather than feeling embarrassed, instead, I felt myself relax. I did take that breath.

"Okay. But let me get my purse so I can check my messages. I should see if anything exploded while I was so distracted last night."

He chuckled as I left the room.

My purse was right where I'd left it on the sofa. I pulled out my phone and meandered back into the kitchen. Nine texts and two missed calls. I sighed.

One call and two texts from Thomas, and the rest from Tessa. I wasn't sure I even wanted to look at them.

"Everything okay?"

"I don't know. The guy from last night..." I held the phone up.

"Maybe he's apologizing."

Maybe he was. I had a look. They *were* all apologies. He didn't know what had happened. He hoped we could at least be friends, etc, etc. The ones from Tessa were mostly asking what the hell had happened. I guessed Thomas called her, freaking out. Her last two texts were *her* freaking out because I wasn't responding. I didn't even want to listen to the voice mails. I'd call her later.

"Well?" Evan raised his mug to his lips.

"Yes. Apologies."

"That was responsible of him."

"I suppose." I dropped the phone back into my purse. "I don't really want to think about it right now. What's on your agenda for today?"

"Actually, the last permits came through for the building yesterday. I have meetings all day with the general contractor and several of the subcontractors. And then we're heading out to the site in the afternoon." He watched me for a second, then asked, "Would you like to see the raw location for the new Helping Hands building?"

I thought about it. Spending more time with Evan would be great—really great, actually, judging by the fluttering in my tummy that I was trying to ignore. But I wasn't sure I wanted to cut into my workday. I said as much.

"How about lunch then? After, you can swing by the site with me so you can have a look-see, then go straight back to the office. I'll bet Annette and Jessie would love to hear about it."

"Okay, lunch is good. I would like to have a peek. Even though I don't really know anything about construction or what's going on, I'm still very interested."

"Great. I'll text you when I have an idea of how long my meetings are going. I'm thinking probably one-ish. Is that too late for you?"

"Nope. That's fine." I really was interested in the site. I mean, I was more interested in a person than the location, yes. But I likely would have gone to the site even if I didn't want to fuck the architect.

-•»«•-

I made it to the office in time for my first client meeting, and the morning flew by. Evan had texted me a specific time and the restaurant. It was a diner about four blocks away that I'd never actually gone to. It had seemed sort of dive-y.

I was just heading out when my cell rang. I was ready to flip it to voice mail if it was Thomas, but it was Tessa. I probably needed to go ahead and talk to her. I'd planned to call after the site visit anyway. Her voice mail had been almost frantic, and I probably should have called her first thing after leaving Evan's. I'm a bad best friend.

"Oh for fuck's sake and thank fucking God," she said when I answered. That's really how I knew she'd been out of her mind with worry. Tessa hardly ever dropped the f-bomb. "I swear, I am going to slap you the next time I see you. I thought you were dead!"

"You're listed as my emergency contact. If I were dead, someone would have called."

"That's not even funny."

I laughed—because it really *was* funny—and stepped out onto the busy sidewalk.

"So what the hell happened last night?"

Evan's dimple flashed through my mind, but that wasn't what Tess was talking about, since she didn't know about Evan. And certainly she didn't know about how it felt like more than a quick fling. "I tried to let Thomas down easy, and he just didn't want to be let down easy."

"That's not what I meant. Well, yes, I meant that too, but honestly...where were you?"

"Oh." I hadn't even thought about how to explain. What to say? "I had a booty call after the date, because I was annoyed." Not entirely untrue.

There was silence on the line, and I thought, almost with relief, that I'd lost her. But then she said, "I call bullshit."

"What?"

"You heard me. Bullshit. You don't do sleepovers. And you would have texted me afterward anyway."

"My phone died?" Sometimes I wished she didn't know me so well.

"Again, bullshit. So where were you?"

I sighed, not sure what to tell her about Evan. "I met this guy a couple weeks ago."

"And you had an overnighter?" The surprise came through in her very loud tone. Very loud.

"Are you at school?"

"Of course I'm at school. Where else would I be?"

"Can you please not talk about my sex life while you're sitting among kindergartners?"

"Don't be dumb. I'm not in my classroom. And stop trying to change the subject."

"Yes, I had an overnighter. What's the problem?" I turned the corner and started down the road that would take me to the diner. Three blocks.

"It's not a problem." She paused, and her voice came across lower. "It's just out of the ordinary for you. Honestly, it hadn't even crossed my mind that you were with a guy. I mean, I knew you might be with someone, but you don't *do* overnighters, and when I hadn't even gotten a text by this morning... Well, that worried me."

"I know. I'm sorry. The thing with Thomas last night weirded me out a bit, and...I guess I just needed company for a while. I wasn't intending on staying overnight."

"Okay, so who is he?"

One block down, two to go. I wasn't sure if I wanted to tell her exactly who Evan was. And that was strange, because I'd never really kept anything from Tessa. Maybe I wanted to hoard Evan all to myself for a little while longer. "I first met him at the bar by my house."

"Chemistry?"

"We only chatted for a minute that first time." He'd completely shut me down. Yeah, I wasn't telling her that. "And we've just run into each other several times since. I'm actually on my way to lunch with him."

"Ohhhh. A lunch quickie?" Lecherousness totally came out in her voice. It made me laugh because Tessa was sort of the stereotype of the kindergarten teacher: young, cute, innocent-looking.

"No, nothing like that." Not that it hadn't crossed my mind. One block left.

"Dang." That was Tessa. Not "damn." But "dang." "What's his name?"

"Evan."

"That's a good name. Strong. Masculine." She paused. Then she said, "*Is* he strong? And masculine?"

"Yes, Tessa, he is strong and masculine." I couldn't help laughing again.

"And is it serious?"

My belly clenched in a quick panic. Why was I having so much trouble talking to her about Evan? Why would she even think there was something serious anyway? Was it serious? Whatever the answer—and really, didn't I already know what it was?—I wasn't ready to put it in words. "We hardly know each other, Tess."

"Well, you blew Thomas off for him."

"I didn't blow Thomas off. There wasn't anything there between me and Thomas."

"But you like this new guy, right?"

I hesitated. And I realized that, yes, I really did like this new guy. I could put that into words. "I do like him."

She gave a happy sigh. "So when do I get details?"

*Meh.* "Well, not now. I am just getting to the restaurant. Let's get together this weekend."

"Okay, it's a date. Have fun!"

"Thanks, doll."

We clicked off, and I slid my phone into my purse. It occurred to me that this was the first real date Evan and I had been on. Well, except that other lunch that ended very, very badly. That didn't count. Anything that ends badly shouldn't count.

I pulled open the door to the diner with *"I do like him"* still in my ears and butterflies in my belly.

*Here we go.*

---

Evan wasn't there when I went in, so I took a booth against the window, near the corner. The place was...old. That was the only real way to describe it. It had the classic diner feel with red vinyl upholstered seats and metal, bolted-down stools at the counter. There was even a jukebox in the far corner that currently played an Elvis tune. But the sound coming from the speakers was scratchy, and every seat in the house looked to have a tear in the vinyl, letting the white stuffing poke out. The linoleum floor looked like it had been black-and-white checkered in the past, but now it was just varying shades of dingy gray.

For as rough as it looked, though, the smells coming from the kitchen were amazing. There were still quite a few people in the booths along with two businessmen and a student—judging from the backpack—finishing up their meals at the counter.

I pulled a menu from the holder behind the napkin box. Pictures and descriptions of breakfast, lunch, and dinner. Lots of eggs and bacon in all the sections. I tried to eat healthy most the time. And the menu did give a nod to lower-calorie stuff in the salad section. But nowhere else.

I decided on a patty melt and fries. To hell with healthy today.

The waitress came up, wearing a typical diner-waitress dress with a white apron and a red nametag that spelled out *Alison*. Her hair was swept back in a bun, and she was very pretty. A bit older than me, but she didn't look run-down, as if she'd been waiting tables all her life. Maybe that was just a stereotype in my own head, though.

Alison pulled a little pad from her apron and gave me a friendly nod. "Afternoon. Know what you're having?"

"Just coffee right now. I'm waiting for someone."

"Gotcha. Back in a shake."

I grinned, mostly to myself. I almost felt like I was in a movie. It was kind of quaint.

Alison brought my coffee just as the bell over the door rang and Evan stepped in. When she looked over and nodded, it was obvious they knew each other. "Evan, good to see you." She stepped from the table so he could slide into the seat across from me.

"It's good to be seen. I hadn't been in for a while, so I thought we'd get lunch here."

"Great." She looked at me and smiled again, the quality different now. No longer just the welcome-to-our-restaurant smile. It was more personal. She turned her attention back to him. "New girl?"

"Perhaps. Too soon to tell." He tipped me a wink. I couldn't decide whether I should be offended. I probably could have been if I felt like ending this lunch in anger like I did before.

Alison gave a soft laugh and touched my shoulder. "Don't mean to talk about you like you're not here. I just have an unhealthy interest in his love life." Her tone conveyed self-deprecation. She looked back at Evan. "Bring you some coffee in a min. Usual, hon?"

"Please. Caly, do you know what you'd like?"

I ordered the patty melt and fries, and Alison left.

"New girl, huh?" I lifted a brow.

Evan laughed. "Alison and I have known each other for a long time. We have history."

"Do you, now?" I doctored up my coffee, thinking it would be interesting to have the shoe on the other foot and maybe throw him off-kilter. Now I was enjoying the conversation. Was it too much to hope that I could put him off his game for once?

"Yes."

Alison returned with his cup of coffee and then disappeared again.

Evan resumed. "We run in the same social circles."

That sort of broke my brain a little bit. "Seriously? A high-profile architect and a waitress? You guys hang out with the same crowd?"

Evan lifted a shoulder in a half shrug. "Stranger things have happened. Though I'd mention that she's more than a waitress."

"What do you mean?"

"She owns the diner. Not that it would matter as far as the social things. But just to be clear." He drank his coffee.

I looked at Alison again as she stood at the counter, chatting with the student there. They both laughed, and she refilled his soda. "Well, even if she is the owner too, it still surprises me that you hang out."

Evan just looked amused. I couldn't decide whether he was being condescending or not.

"Is she part of the game as well?" I wasn't sure why I made that connection, but why not, right?

"Well, not part of my game. She plays her own." He raised his cup to his lips, sipped, and then said, "We all do, though."

That was true.

One of the things about diners is that the food comes out superfast, and this place was no exception. Alison set our plates down in front of us, and the smells wafting off those things were amazing. My mouth watered, and I was grateful I had the food in front of me, because I wasn't sure I'd be able to keep from eating off someone else's plate.

Evan's "usual" was meatloaf cozied up with some mashed potatoes and baby carrots. I looked from his plate to his face.

"I didn't really peg you for a meatloaf guy," I said after Alison left.

He had already set about cutting his food. "There are meatloaf guys?"

"You know. It seems like a down-home sort of meal. You struck me more as an escargot and chardonnay kind of guy." Of course, last time I'd seen escargot, I'd been out with Thomas. I pushed that away.

"Are you kidding me? I grew up on meat and potatoes." As if to emphasize, he shoved a forkful of both in his mouth and grinned.

"Well, apparently I need to reassess my idea of you." I took a bite of my patty melt. "Oh my God." Okay, so I talked with my mouth full. Sue me. I waited until I'd chewed and swallowed before uttering my follow-up. "That is fucking incredible. How have I never been to this place with the food of the gods?"

Evan laughed. "Probably looked too much like a hole-in-the-wall to you. Snooty lawyer and all."

I threw my napkin at him.

—➤➤◄◄—

And that was how lunch went. Easy. Low-key. No arguing, no anger. It was nice. After we'd eaten and paid, he asked if I was ready to see the build site. I scooted out of the booth and straightened my skirt.

"You look very nice today, by the way."

I tried not to flush—because I shouldn't care that a man complimented me—but I flushed anyway. "Thank you."

As he held the door open for me, he whispered, "Maybe one day we'll make you a rope bra for underneath."

I coughed out a laugh. "You're naughty."

"Yes." He put his hand on the small of my back and guided me onto the sidewalk. "It's about five blocks. We can take a cab, if you'd rather not walk in your heels."

I looked at him and hoped my expression conveyed the idea that what he'd just said was stupid. "I spend eight to ten hours a day in these heels. Some days even longer. Five blocks isn't going to kill me."

He held up both hands in mock surrender. "All right. I have been duly chastised."

"Does that mean I get to spank you?"

He threw back his head and let out what could only be termed a guffaw. "Absolutely not."

"You sure? You might enjoy it." I waggled my brows at him.

"Please be assured that I do not enjoy it."

"So you've been on the receiving end?"

"I've tried it, yes. It's not to my liking."

"Because it hurts!"

"Yes, it does, but the pain isn't really the issue. True enough that it doesn't do anything for me except get me annoyed. But the issue with being on the bottom side of any of those sorts of games is more about the control."

I marveled at how quickly the conversation went from teasing and being silly to being very serious. I raised my voice to be heard over the transit bus that had stopped on the street just behind us. "You don't like not to have it. Control, I mean."

"Exactly right."

We dropped into silence for a moment, and I listened to the traffic as we continued up the street. I started making some connections. "So tell me about these social circles that you and Alison frequent together."

"We don't really frequent them together, so much as we are sometimes at the same place at the same time."

"So she was never one of your 'new girls'?" I put a teasing emphasis on the phrase, and he peered at me from the corner of his eye.

"She actually was, once, briefly. But we realized pretty early that it wouldn't work for us."

"Why not? She seems pretty enough."

"It's not about beauty."

"Thanks."

Another sidelong look. "Beauty is fluid, and beauty comes and goes. Even for a single person. Someone who is not considered traditionally beautiful by society's standards can transform into the sort of beauty you can't capture in a photo or see on a screen. So beauty is not a heavily weighted factor, since it is transient."

I was dubious. Apparently it showed on my face.

"Of course, *attraction* is important. And if you equate attraction with beauty, then I suppose an argument can be made for beauty. But, again, that's not the important bit."

"So what is?"

We turned a corner and began trudging up a hill.

"My need for control must have a counter. A yang to my yin."

"Waxing poetic?"

"No. It's true."

"So you mean that you need to have control, so therefore you need someone who...needs to be controlled?" My hackles came up a little bit, because what did that say about me? But I wanted to hear what he had to say before I flipped out about how women are not children and everyone should be in control of their own lives.

"And there's where it gets complicated. When you say 'someone who needs to be controlled,' you're likely thinking of some broken woman who can't make a decision for herself because she's only ever had men in her life who kept her beaten down. Perhaps maybe not quite that extreme, but some version of that. Am I near the mark?"

He was pretty much right on top of the mark. "Yes. People who can't take control of their lives strike me as weak." Sure, there were always extenuating circumstances in some cases—medical issues that we obviously can't control comes to mind—but for the most part, what I said was my belief.

"And that's where it gets tricky. Because there's a big difference between 'can't take control' and 'chooses to cede control.'" He didn't say anything more right away.

I let those words bounce around in my head. "Why would someone choose to cede control? I mean, I struggled and fought to get where I am today. I couldn't imagine giving that up."

"Why would you feel you had to give it up?"

Okay, I admit, I was thinking of a woman kept barefoot and pregnant in the kitchen. But I didn't tell him that.

"Why couldn't you still be the high-powered lawyer at the premier law firm in the city?"

"I don't understand."

"See? It can be complicated."

We turned another corner, and Evan pointed about three quarters of a block up. "There it is."

Ahead, a mostly empty lot took up most of the block. It was obvious a building had come down. There was still a foundation, and there was rubble scattered about. Old, worn beams of wood were piled up at the other side of the lot not too far from a metal trailer that was obviously the construction office. Three men stood outside it, one in a business suit and the other two in jeans and work shirts. As we approached, I realized that Brad Crenshaw was the one in the suit.

Ugh. What would he say about me arriving with the architect?

"The guy next to Brad in the blue shirt is my general contractor, James. The other guy is his assistant, Tony. You won't have to remember their names or anything, though if you visit the site, you'll likely see James again."

"I remember James from that meeting last week."

"Oh yes. He was there. That's right."

When we approached, Evan did introductions, his hand on the small of my back the entire time. Once we'd gotten that out of the way, the men gave Evan their report and the general timing of the build plan. Brad kept eyeing me sidelong. His questions may as well have been written all over his face. But that didn't matter, since the answers were none of his business. Even if he was one of the name partners.

My instinct was always to protect my privacy. But I wondered if that had to do with the fact that I'm basically a love-'em-and-leave-'em kind of girl. There's a certain amount of social stigma attached to that. I made a mental note to add a section about that to my book.

We all went into the trailer—which was definitely a little tight with five of us in there—and they pulled out schematics and blueprints. Evan never moved from my side, even as they started talking serious building. I wondered how it would be, moving through life with him like this.

And where the hell had *that* come from?

"I'm going to head back," I said to Evan. When freaked out, run.

Brad gave me a nod, but I pretended I didn't see it.

"Oh, I'm sorry. I probably should have warned you that it wouldn't be very exciting." Evan tipped me a wink that sent butterflies through my entire system. I cleared my throat.

"No, it's fine. I just have a lot of work on my desk, so it's better for me to go ahead."

"Let me walk you out."

We left the trailer and went to the pavement, where Evan hailed a cab, even though I was fine to walk.

"I brought you twice as far in the opposite direction and some of these side streets are not the safest. I'd feel better if you took a cab," he said as he held the door open for me, ever the sexy gentleman. "I'll call you later."

I spent the whole cab ride thinking about the waitress and the games and the idea of controlling someone without turning the person into a not-person. I still didn't understand the appeal of letting someone take over. I mean, sure, it made my lady bits tingle with Evan, but the idea of handing over that sort of control on a larger scale… Well, it just seemed weird.

Work went by quickly because I got involved in writing case notes and looking up precedents. Before I knew it, it was six and the support staff were all leaving.

At seven thirty, my phone rang, and I had to pull my nose out of the book—okay, the screen—to answer. It was Evan. My heart fluttered a little. "Hello."

"I didn't mean to seem as if I was ditching you this afternoon," he said.

"I didn't feel ditched. You offered me a chance to see the site, and I saw it. I'm sure it will look better once you guys do your magic on it."

"I hope so. It would be a blow to my ego to think you would be less impressed when we were finished than when we began."

Was it charming that he seemed to care what I thought? Yes. Yes, it was.

"Are you at home?"

"No, I'm still at the office." I started sorting papers into "stay at the office" and "take home" piles.

"Have you eaten?"

"I had some takeout earlier."

"Good. You and I are alike, I think, in that when we get involved in our work, we sometimes forget to do the normal stuff we should be doing to take care of ourselves."

I didn't tell him that the only reason I ordered takeout was because my assistant reminded me I needed to eat. "Yep. Guilty."

"I think I'm going to stop by Chemistry on my way home, if you want to grab a drink with me later. I live a sad life. I will have bid proposals scattered all over the table while I drink my Evan Williams."

I laughed. "We'll see. I've got a few more things to do here before I'm out." I wasn't really sure I wanted to meet him. Even though I liked spending time together—seriously, no one else made my heart flutter—maybe I was spending too much time. Although I still wanted to finish that conversation about control. I had a lot of questions.

"Excellent. Be productive."

"You too."

—➤➤◄◄—

By the time I got done at the office, I was pretty exhausted. But bits and pieces of the conversation with Evan kept flitting through my brain. It was after ten, but I stopped into Chemistry anyway, on the off chance that he hadn't made it home yet.

And he hadn't.

He was at one of the booths and, as promised, had all sorts of papers strewn across the table's surface. On the corner was a short glass with a finger or two of what I assumed was his bourbon. I watched him for a minute as he pored over the table, his expression tight with concentration. His thick eyebrows drew together and then relaxed as he shuffled through papers to find the one he wanted. He jotted down a few notes and moved on to another paper.

"Caly!" Jason, the bartender, flashed his very white teeth at me. He was a nice kid. An actor, if I remembered correctly. "I haven't seen you in here for a while. Lemon drop?"

That was my hunting drink. "No. How about an amaretto sour, instead?"

"Ooohh. Changing it up. Gotcha."

"I'll be at that booth over there." I motioned to where Evan sat. Jason nodded and I walked over. "Hey you."

Evan looked up at me, and his eyes lit up with his smile. "Hey, yourself." He started shuffling papers, to clear off the other half of the table. "Sit. Sit."

I slid into the booth, my satchel on my shoulder. "You look busy."

"Yeah, some last-minute changes to the plans. We've got to get them through the permit office." He glanced at his watch, and his brows went up. "You worked late too."

"Yeah." As if on cue, I yawned. "Long day."

"Tell me about it." Evan leaned back against the wooden planks of the booth bench just as Jason dropped my drink off.

"Want to start a tab, Cal?" Jason asked.

"Just put it on mine," Evan said.

Jason winked at me and went back to the bar.

"Thanks for the drink," I said. "It seems a common practice with us that we get together and you get me liquored up."

He barked out a laugh. "Yeah, that's me. Have to ply women with alcohol to get them to spend time with me."

I grinned, raised my glass to him, and then took a sip. Tart and sweet at the same time. My favorite combination.

"No lemon drop?"

"Nope. Not tonight."

"I see."

"This will probably be my only drink anyway. I'm about ready to sack out."

He nodded.

"I want you to talk more, though. About the control thing."

Evan arranged the papers into stacks. "Sure. What specifically?" He slid some into folders and others he clipped into bundles before putting all of them into his briefcase.

"You said it was complicated. And that someone wouldn't necessarily have to quit a job or give up things she's achieved just because she...how did you put it? Ceded control to someone else."

"Yes."

"Explain, please."

Evan brought the glass to his lips and sipped, his gaze thoughtful. "One of the things that I enjoy about being in control is the power it brings. Not necessarily power over a specific person—though there is that too—but the inherent power in having dominion over someone, having control of *their* power. Does that make sense?"

"I suppose."

"But how much power I would have depends entirely on the power of the person I control. And this is personal power I'm talking about. Not political power or financial power. This is strictly the power of the person. If I had control over someone weak, someone who essentially would bow to *anyone* else's control, then how much power does that really give me? There is no power to be granted to me if she does not have personal power in her own right."

Something niggled in the back of my head, but I couldn't quite put my finger on what it was. "So...what you want is to have some woman of power under your thumb."

"Yes." He looked me straight in the eye. "If she wants to be under my thumb."

And, of course, then it hit me. "That's why you went after me. You see me as a woman of power and you want me under your thumb."

He gave that annoying cryptic grin. "Only if you wanted to be under my thumb."

I fought with myself about whether I wanted to just get up and leave. What a fucked-up thing! I didn't really know what I wanted out of whatever it was we were doing, but he obviously knew exactly what he wanted out of it. He wanted a puppet. Some little slave girl who would do his bidding. Something kept me sitting, though. Whether it was some connection to him I didn't want to sever, or whether it was just incredulity at how crazy this all sounded, I had no idea.

"Caly," he said, leaning forward, putting his forearms on the table, "it's not an insult. It's not that I think you're an easy mark, or that I want to take advantage of you. Do you understand that?"

I gave him my best steely gaze and didn't answer.

"It's because I find you intriguing and beautiful and powerful. And I feel a pull from you. I feel a need in you that matches a need in me. Whether that's wanting to cede control, I don't know. I can't claim to know you that well. But there's something there, and it's something I'm interested in exploring."

I still didn't respond. I was stewing, but at the same time, I knew he was being honest and forthright. There was something to be said for that. Plus, he was right. There *was* something there between us. I just didn't know what it was either.

He killed the last of his drink. "I told you that we play different games. And we do. We have different rules. One of the differences is that I'm being completely honest about why I'm doing what I'm doing. And you have control over whether you do it with me." He pulled his wallet out and fished out a twenty. He dropped it on the table and then took his briefcase in hand. "I'm not going to ask you back to my place tonight. But I will again soon. And I hope you decide that you're interested in exploring and learning my game. Because I think we would both have a very good time."

I wanted to stop him, but I didn't have anything to stop him with. I mean, I could have offered to go home with him and, to be honest, a part of me wanted to. But the rest of me was still tripping over what he'd said and trying to make sense of it. So I watched him stand and take a couple steps toward me. He leaned down and kissed the top of my head.

"Be careful getting home."

And then he was gone.

# Chapter Twelve

I didn't sleep. Well, maybe two hours, but that was pretty much the same as not sleeping at all. I decided to call in to work, because I was a zombie. I wouldn't be very worthwhile. And then I phoned Tessa.

"Are you free for coffee this afternoon?"

"Sure. This is sooner than I expected."

"I need to talk to you about this guy."

There was silence for half a second, and then she said, "Ookay. Are you all right?"

"Yes, I'm fine. I just… He has this ability to put me out of sorts. I think I need a sounding board. I just need to talk about it a bit."

"All right. I'll have all the kids on the buses by one." Being a kindergarten teacher gave Tessa a little more flextime.

"That would be perfect. I'm not going in to work today, so I'll be by to pick you up when you're off."

"You're freaking me out a little bit, you know that?"

"Don't feel bad. I'm freaking me out a lot. So you're in good company."

--→→←←--

Tessa waited for me at the front door of her school. Her red hair was piled haphazardly on top of her head and the cat-eye shades she wore made her look like she should be wearing a poodle skirt, not the khaki slacks and light summer sweater she was wearing. She still used the old patchwork backpack I'd made her in college. It was some weird textile construction class I'd taken as an elective because I thought it would be interesting and cool. Turned out that I hate sewing. Who knew?

She hopped in the car and tossed the backpack on the floor. "Hey! I miss you."

"I'm here now." I pulled out of the school parking lot and headed a few miles east toward a small indie coffee shop called the Daily Grind.

"Thomas wasn't the guy, huh?"

"No, he really wasn't."

"Did he have a third nipple or something?"

I sputtered a laugh. "I have no idea how many nipples the man has."

"He seemed so your type."

"I have a type? When have you ever seen me in a relationship?"

"Well, yeah, there is that. So tell me about this dude."

I told her about meeting Evan at Chemistry—still left out the part about him shutting me down—then meeting again at the formal party.

Tessa smacked me on the leg. "It's like a Sandra Bullock movie! I love this."

All things pop culture. That was my Tessa.

She and I had been best friends since college, even though I was from hippie stock and she was a boarding-school rich kid. They'd paired us up as roommates sophomore year and after a rocky first month that resulted in black eyes for both of us, we ended up joined at the hip.

She knew my theories on getting men into bed, and she was really the first one who told me I was commitment-phobic. I told her to mind her own damned business. So, naturally, she found this whole story about Evan compelling in such a way that I was sure she was already helping me pick out wedding dresses in her head.

At least, until I got to the rope...and then the spanking.

"Oh my God. He's kinky! Just like that book."

I'd heard about the book, of course, read an excerpt or two, and refused to read any more on the basis that I liked my brain cells alive, thank you very much. But Tessa had read them all.

"I guess he is. But there seems to be more than just kinky sex."

"What do you mean?"

By then, we'd gotten to the Grind, and so I paused the conversation while we waited in line and then ordered. When we were safely at a table in a corner, I told her about the conversation I'd had with Evan about control.

"Oh! He wants to pull your hair while you're giving him a blowjob."

Thinking about the fact that he *hadn't* pulled my hair while I gave him a blowjob, I shook my head. "Like I said, I think it's more than that. The conversation we had today didn't have anything to do with sex. It was about power and control. Apparently there are women who like to give up control to men. I guess the other way around would work too. Or same sex. But we were really talking about me and him. I think. Anyway, when I said I couldn't imagine giving up the things that I'd worked for, he asked me why I thought I would have to. And I don't get that. Isn't that what controlling means? Another person gets to decide what I do?"

"Maybe. But obviously he doesn't see that as a bad thing. So maybe we don't get what the situation really looks like. Realistically, if you gave control over your life to someone else, you would have to trust him, right? I mean, you wouldn't give someone that much power over you just on a whim. Just because he gets your juices flowing."

I've always considered myself pretty damn smart. Tessa could run circles around me, though, once she got her thinking cap on. And she had that cap on tight today.

"Yes, that makes sense," I said. "I wouldn't just give it to some dude. He'd have to be committed to making sure I was taken care of. I don't mean money-wise either. I can do that, obviously. I mean mentally, physically. But how fulfilling could that possibly be?"

"It's not really all that much different than traditional, old-fashioned marriage roles. I mean, it could go with any gender pairing or whatever, but one person is the boss and the other person is..."

"June Cleaver? Because I seem so much like June Cleaver." I crossed my eyes at her.

Tessa laughed. One of my favorite things about her was how easily her laugh came. "Let's just talk in generalities. Let's take me, for instance. If Gordon were like Ward Cleaver, then he'd be the one making the final decisions, right?"

I nodded.

"But he knows how much I love my kids at school. How much I love teaching. Do you think he'd make me quit?"

"Gordon? No. Of course not."

"That's sort of how I'm looking at this whole control thing. I don't know if that's how your mystery guy views it."

"Evan."

"Evan. I don't know if that's how Evan views it, but it makes sense in my head. Teaching makes me happy. It helps to fulfill my life. If Gordon loves me and wants my happiness, why would he not allow that, even if I gave him control over that part of my life?"

Okay, that did make some sense. And that jibed pretty well with what Evan was saying about remaining a high-powered lawyer in a premier firm. "But I still don't get what the draw of it is. For the woman. You. June Cleaver. Whatever."

Tessa shrugged and stirred her latte. The espresso and the milk mingled together into a light brown. "I could see the appeal in feeling protected. Feeling safe. I can see that feeling going hand in hand with the trust part. If you trust someone to that level—the level that your happiness and your safety are in his hands—and he consistently comes through. I can totally see the draw of that."

"I hadn't thought of it that way."

She bowed her head for a moment. "Tessa Walcott. Opening minds to new ways of thinking since 1981!"

I cracked up. "Okay. So the whole thing doesn't seem quite so...demeaning coming from the angle you're talking about. He made it very clear last night that he's interested in that sort of situation with me."

"He wants to control your life?"

"I don't know. I just… I don't know exactly what that means. We fooled around–"

"Did you fuck him?" Tessa's voice was quiet but high-pitched.

"We haven't fucked, no. But we've done other things."

"Oooh. Like what?" Tessa had always liked living vicariously through me. She and Gordon lived a pretty quiet life, and they liked it that way, both of them. But hearing my stories scratched a tiny itch in Tessa. Better for me to scratch it than her to scratch it.

"Can we talk about that later? Like maybe when we're not in the middle of a crowd of soccer moms?"

She pouted. "Fine."

"Anyway, we fooled around, and he definitely did some controlling things." I thought about all the interactions I'd had with Evan since we first met. "Hmm. You know what I'm noticing?"

"What's that?"

"I'd recognized it very early on, but then I forgot, because he keeps me so off balance. He always wants to know if I'm willing to do something. Like, he phrases it that way. 'Will you...whatever?'"

"Interesting. I think that's good. It means he cares what you want, I think. He wants you to be doing these things of your own free will."

I nodded again, slowly. My brain was moving. "He said that he wants to explore whatever it is we've got going on right now. I'm not sure I'm ready for that."

Tessa took a sip of her coffee. "Isn't that what you're already doing?"

*Guh.* I hated it when she pointed shit like this out to me: the obvious that I don't see even when it's right in front of my face. "Sometimes you make me crazy."

"I know. It's a gift."

I rolled my eyes. "So you think I should do it?"

"Are you having fun?"

I thought about that. "When I'm not wanting to strangle him. Although, truth be told, the urge to strangle him has been less common since we've been having sexy times."

Tessa grinned. "Of course. So you are having fun."

"Yes, I guess I am."

"Then why would you stop?"

Tessa's logic never failed to halt me in my tracks.

"It's not like it's forever. If you stop having fun, you can walk away."

"I'm still freaked out by the whole control thing."

"Do you think he'll try to take control of things you don't allow? Is it that you're afraid he's going to start bossing you around and telling you who you can talk to, who you can have dinner with?"

I met her gaze. "Shouldn't I be afraid of that?"

"Only if you really think that's what he would do. Has he seemed like that sort?"

"I don't know. Does any man seem that sort at the beginning? I don't think I know him well enough. He's only done things I've given him permission to do. Well, some of the kinky stuff I didn't give express permission for, but I understood he was going to do stuff I wasn't anticipating. I never felt like he was going to rape me or anything." Especially since it took forever just to get him to let me touch his damned cock.

"If he were some guy who was making demands on you, I would tell you to run in the other direction. But that's not what I'm getting from the things you're telling me. It *sounds* like he's wanting you to be on board for each step he wants to take. That makes me feel like your wants and needs are important to him, even though he wants to drive the car. Does that make sense?"

"Yes. So I should call him up and say, 'Hey, Evan, I'm ready to be your sex slave now!'?"

Tessa let out a loud, high-pitched laugh that brought the attention of a couple of the folks at the surrounding tables. She didn't even notice. She never did. I love her a lot. "I guess you could. But maybe it would be better just to play it by ear. Go with the flow for as long as you feel comfortable."

I nodded but didn't respond. I suddenly had hit the limit of how much I wanted to talk about the whole control and relationship thing. I felt overwhelmed again, but at least I wasn't as off-kilter as I had been. Everything seemed a little more clear in my head, but I was just tired of thinking about it.

Tessa, who sometimes seemed like a mind reader, said, "So are you going to share the naughty details, or do I have to make them up for myself?"

I chuckled. "Always the voyeur."

She leaned back in her chair and raised her mug. "You know it."

-->>><<--

I didn't call Evan that day. Or the next. I begged out of going to the groundbreaking ceremony on Thursday. I told Annette I just wasn't feeling up to it. I didn't go into detail. And that was the truth too. I really *wasn't* feeling up to it.

Evan sent me a text on Friday checking on me. I responded that I was fine and I'd talk to him later in the weekend. I just needed some space. He seemed to understand, because he didn't push. In the meantime, I threw myself into my caseload and made plans to spend the weekend working at Helping Hands. I considered asking Evan if he was volunteering, but then I couldn't work out whether I wanted his answer to be yes or no. So I decided I'd deal with him if he showed up.

Tessa called every day, also to check on me. Every time she asked if I'd spoken to Evan, she sighed at my response. When I told her on Saturday morning that he and I had texted Friday, she seemed overjoyed.

"By the way," she said, "when do I get to meet him?"

"How about one thing at a time? How about I decide whether I want to continue seeing him first?"

"I thought that was already decided."

She was right that I'd started backtracking after our conversation at the coffee shop. I'd started second-guessing what she and I had talked about and the tentative decision I'd made that afternoon. "I'm just taking some time to think."

"Your problem is that you overthink. I swear, for being the spontaneous one, you get in your own damn way too often."

"Fine. I'll call him later."

"When?"

"When I get done at the shelter."

"Do I have to follow up with you to make sure you did it?"

"Are you matchmaking again?"

"No. This is all you. I'm just...encouraging." I could hear her smart-ass smirk through the phone.

"Oy."

When we got off the line, I finished dressing and went over to Helping Hands. I realized I hadn't been there since the weekend before and that seemed like a long time. I was usually in and out several times a week. Annette grabbed me in her arms and pulled me into a bear hug.

"Caly! I've missed you!"

I disentangled myself. "I was just here last weekend."

She gave me a wink. "I know. But we're used to seeing you more often. You must have had a busy week." She elbowed me.

"Are you seriously giving me the wink-wink, nudge-nudge thing?"

"Yep. Exactly what I'm doing. We missed you at the ground breaking. It was really lovely! Your beau was there." She grinned at me.

"My beau?"

"Yes."

I took a deep breath. "I'm not even going to pretend I don't know who you think my beau is. And I'm not surprised he was there. He is the one doing the building, after all."

Annette looked vaguely annoyed at not being able to verbally poke me a little, but it was a good-natured annoyed. She flashed her bright smile and said, "I think he missed you too."

I just shook my head and walked to the back. I couldn't keep myself from scanning the faces of the volunteers for Evan. But he didn't seem to be there. I had the strange combined feeling of being both relieved and disappointed.

------>>><<<----

I ended up bugging out right after dinner, leaving the other volunteers to the cleanup. I'd spent the entire time flipping over in my mind what Evan had said and what Tessa had said. And then there was what I wanted—which seemed pretty damned elusive.

I liked Evan. More than I'd really allowed myself to like any man since before college. And that was weird in and of itself. I kept replaying Tessa's question to me. Was I having fun?

Aside from the times when we ended up in fights—which actually wasn't often and, if I was being *really* honest, was more about me running than anything—I actually was having fun. A lot of it even.

I wanted more fun.

We hadn't even fucked yet. Everything so far had been explosive. What would happen when we got down to serious business?

By the time dinner service was done, I'd decided I was going to Evan's place and let him know I was along for the ride. We'd see where this little out-of-control train was gonna go.

Of course, by the time I'd actually gone home, showered, got in my car, and drove to his house, I'd made myself crazy with the second-guessing. I circled his block once, checking to see if he was home. His BMW sat in the driveway.

As I approached again, I slowed and stopped just before his mailbox. His house looked quiet. I put the car in Park.

"If I pull into that driveway, that's it. I'm committed. I mean, he'll have heard the car and come to look. He'd see me sitting in the driveway talking to myself like an idiot— because apparently that's my thing right now. I'm sure I look much more sane sitting on the street, talking to myself, staring at his house like some bunny-cooking stalker. Maybe I should just call him." I searched through my purse for my phone.

Taking it out didn't really help. "What do I say when he answers? 'Oh, hey, look out your window.' Wave. Yeah, then he'll just flip over to a second line and dial 911. Crazy lady outside my house." I wrinkled my nose at myself. "I really do sound crazy. I can't believe I'm sitting here having this conversation with myself. Obviously this is not something I'm ready to do just y—"

A knock at the window.

I just about jumped out of my skin. I looked to my left and there he was.

Evan stood next to my car, wifebeater shirt stretched across his chest, hair dark with sweat. He waved at me.

I was an idiot.

# Chapter Thirteen

I rolled down my window and tried to laugh. It came out more like a frog choking on a fly. "Hey."

And there came the dimple. "Hey, yourself."

"So…you're not in your house." Because I'm a lawyer, and I'm smart.

"No. I went out for a run." He watched me as I tried to figure out what the hell to say. "You know you didn't quite make it to the driveway." He pointed past his mailbox to the house.

"Yeah."

"Do you want to pull in so there's a shorter walk to the door?" His grin made me think he knew exactly what was going on in my head. As if he knew I'd been sitting there talking to myself like the world's craziest woman. Maybe he'd watched me for a while before he knocked on the window.

"Yeah, that might be good."

"I'll meet you up there." He took off at a jog, and I leaned my head forward and banged it methodically against the steering wheel.

"I am such an idiot. I am such an idiot."

---

He'd left the kitchen door open for me, but he was nowhere to be seen. I wandered into the living room and heard sounds coming from the hallway.

"Did you finally make it inside?" he called.

"Yes."

"I'm going to grab a shower. There's some iced tea in the fridge, if you want some. I'll be out in ten."

"Thanks." I thought about his sweaty body under the cascading water of the shower and thought briefly about joining him. My pulse thrummed in my veins. "Okay, Caly, get a grip." I went back into the kitchen and poured myself some tea. Then, as an afterthought, I poured another glass for him. I plunked a couple ice cubes into each and went back into the living room.

I'd never really taken stock of the room before. On the back wall—the one shared with the kitchen—three dark wood, floor-to-ceiling bookshelves stood crammed to overflowing with paperbacks and hardbacks.

I set both glasses on coasters on the coffee table and went to check out the books. Lots of classics along the top shelves. Shakespeare, Thoreau, Hemingway. The books didn't seem to be grouped in any specific order, except by very general classifications. Classics, mysteries, science fiction, thrillers. There was a whole shelf devoted to architecture books—not particularly surprising.

The bottom shelf of the one farthest in the corner had some interesting titles: *Kinky Loving; Beat Me, Tie Me;*

*Ropework for Lovers*; *On Her Knees*. They all looked like nonfiction, which I found weird. I would have expected titles like that to be in the porn section and to be novels. The idea that there was nonfiction out there had never really crossed my mind.

I pulled out *Kinky Loving* and paged through. Chapters on sadism and masochism. On bondage. On dominance and submission. On something called domestic discipline. There were a few black-and-white photos sprinkled through the text, but nothing as racy as I'd expected.

I smelled him before I saw him. Cloves and sweetness.

"Find any interesting reading?" I turned around, and he stood there in a pair of shorts, no shirt, toweling his head dry. He draped the towel around his shoulders. "You're welcome to borrow any of them if you wish."

I couldn't find my voice. I think I stammered a little.

He gave a soft chuckle and then turned away. He took one of the glasses from the table. "Thank you for thinking to pour me some tea. I appreciate it." He took a long gulp.

I shoved the book back into its place on the shelf. "You're welcome. How was your run?" Subject change. Yes, that was the answer.

"Not bad. I haven't been to the dojo in a while so I was getting antsy. The run helped."

I nodded and walked away from the bookshelves. Far away.

"You were at the shelter today?" he asked.

"Yes."

"How are the ladies?" He sat on the sofa and motioned me down. I joined him.

"They're fine."

"You know, at the ground breaking, Annette was giving me these sidelong glances and sly grins." He leaned in like he was about to share a secret. "I think she might know I tied you up."

I flushed and laughed. Because even though I was a bit embarrassed about the idea, it was still damn funny. "She was doing the wink-wink, nudge-nudge thing today. Totally admitted to it too." I decided not to share the "beau" comment. For some reason, that one seemed too much.

"At least she's honest." He grinned.

"Yes, I suppose there is that." The tea—which I'd apparently forgotten to drink this whole time—was sweet and cold.

"So what brought you to park by my mailbox this evening?"

I wasn't really sure I wanted to tell him. It's not something I admit often, but I'm not a big share-your-feelings sort of girl, especially with guys. With Tessa, yes. Men? Not so much. I finally took a deep breath. What did I have to lose, really?

"So that whole thing about control that you talked about the other day freaked me out a bit."

He nodded. Like he'd know that. *Pfft.*

"I like you, though. And I don't tend to connect with guys much. Well, except as hookups. Honestly, and no offense, but I don't have much use for your gender, overall."

Evan looked surprised for all of a second, and then he burst into laughter.

I only smiled, because I was trying to figure out why the hell I had even said that. Did I have any control over my mouth at all?

"Yes, I think some of us have very limited applications, so to speak." Evan tilted his head toward me. "But if you want the truth of it, it goes for your gender as well."

"I suppose that is probably true."

Silence blanketed us for a moment, and he waited, just watching me. Nervous energy coiled in my belly. I wasn't sure what else to say. I knew I should be saying something, but I was really at a loss.

"I...I came over because I wanted to talk to you."

"All right. I'm guessing it wasn't to let me know that my gender is mostly useless." The twinkle in his eye matched his grin. The insides uncoiled. The nerves loosened just a bit. I realized the change had something to do with that twinkle.

"No. I..." *Ah, screw it.* I shifted a bit on the sofa so that most of my body faced him. "From what you said the other day, you're interested in controlling me. Is that true?" Sometimes my lawyer-ness can come in handy.

"Yes."

"What does that mean, exactly? Are you wanting to tell me where to go, who to talk to?"

"I suppose it could end up being that way. That's certainly not a starting point."

"But that is what you want?"

He paused for a breath and then took the towel off his shoulders. He draped it over the back of the sofa. "Caly, I can't give you a spreadsheet of what I want. Or a flowchart. It's not as concrete as that. A big part of what I want in relationships of any sort has to do with the person I'm interacting with." He touched my knee with two fingertips. I tried to ignore the tingle. "It's a complicated and beautiful dance. I lead. You follow. I move a certain way, and you mirror it, but add your own flourish. This isn't something that I dictate. We do this together."

I shook my head. "I guess I just don't understand how it happens in a *practical* way. Like what it actually looks like."

"Sometimes, you will offer control. Sometimes I will take it. We may not always talk about it directly, but the option to talk about it directly always exists."

"It's still abstract. I'm a lawyer. I deal in abstract with concrete examples."

"You remember last week when you got upset because I took my cock away from you when you wanted to touch it?"

I nodded. I remembered being angry, but also hurt. Insulted.

"I choose when you touch me. That is my control." The devilish look sneaked into his eye again. "Sexually, I choose when you get your release." I must have projected the shock I felt, because he leaned in and said, "We can work up to that one."

"I don't think I like that."

He shrugged. "You haven't tried it yet."

"I am not sure I want to. When I want an orgasm, I want an orgasm. I'm not going to wait."

"All right." I couldn't read his face, aside from the now overriding look of smugness.

"What do you mean, 'all right'?"

"How many meanings does that phrase have?"

"You're just going to give up on having that control?" I found that hard to believe.

He leaned in very close to me, his nose not even an inch from mine. "The rules of your game don't apply here. In your game, you give chase. In my game, I do no such thing." He leaned back again. "If you aren't interested in playing the game, I'm not going to run after you, hoping you'll change your mind."

This was starting to get annoying.

"Don't mistake me, though. I want you to remain. I want you in the game. But I am not the sort of person who will chase you. I will pursue. I will make my intentions clear. But if you are not choosing to be in this game by your own mind, then I don't want you in it."

"What if I don't like all the rules?"

"Do you want assurances that I wouldn't make you do things you don't want to do?"

"Yes. I think that's probably it."

"I can't make those assurances."

"What?"

"There will be times where you will do things you don't want to do, like the orgasm issue. That's simply part of it. I doubt it will be often, because, from what I believe I understand of you, there will not be too many things you'll be so affronted by that you won't want to do them for me."

"Well you're the arrogant bastard, aren't you?" I was still amazed at how my emotions did all these hard turns around him. Sometimes he had me so frazzled, I didn't know my name. Sometimes he could be such a right asshole that I wanted to punch him. Sometimes he could make me feel like I never wanted to leave his side. It was infuriating.

"I've definitely been labeled that, yes." He spread his hands. "Caly, you're a grown woman. You get to decide whether you want to play this game with me or whether you don't. And you can decide now that you want to play and in three weeks, you can decide you're done playing. I'm not going to force you to stay with me if you wish to go."

"I didn't think you would."

"But I don't think you're convinced that I won't. Because you keep hesitating. You're drawn to the idea, even though you don't know why. You believe I wouldn't force you to stay, but it's still a good excuse to keep from deciding to do it. Because you can't work out exactly why you're attracted to the idea, so your knee jerk is to say no. But you're analytical enough to know that you don't have a logical reason to say no."

"I don't need a reason." My skin was hot. He was getting too close to home.

"Yes, you do. Not for me. But for yourself. Even though you sometimes seem as if you're reacting emotionally—like when you storm out—the emotions are really just a convenient tool to allow you to extricate yourself from a situation you're ready to be done with."

I tried to wrap my head around what he was saying. He was right that my analytical side was strong. But did I do that?

"The basic facts are thus." Who says thus? "You like me. You enjoy our time together. I won't force you to stay if you don't wish to. The only thing truly keeping you from walking this path with me is fear. And you don't want to face that it is fear, because one of the things you pride yourself on is being fearless."

I got to my feet and moved across the room, back to the bookcases. He didn't come after me. He didn't speak.

I tried to unpack what he said. I couldn't find a flaw, a mistake. Even the hardest part—the fact that I was scared— was correct. Tessa had pretty much pointed it out during our conversation without using the actual words.

Fear was something I'd always run from. Sometimes running meant hitting it head-on. Usually it meant rearranging the situation so that the thing I feared was no longer around.

Did I want Evan no longer around?

I stared at the bookshelf in front of me. It was one with a bunch of science fiction on it. I recognized a couple: Asimov, Niven, Bradbury. Some I didn't. Resnick, Heinlein, Kress. I wasn't a big science-fiction reader.

The ice in Evan's tea tinkled behind me. I turned around to see him taking a final sip, emptying the clear glass.

"How would this work?"

He just looked at me for a moment. "What do you mean?"

"This thing." I waved my hand in a vague circle in front of me. "This thing we're talking about. How would it work?"

He gave a soft chuckle and stood, setting the glass on a coaster as he did. He walked around the sofa. I'd be lying if I said I wasn't fighting the urge to move away. Some part of my brain remained detached and very amused at these knee-jerk reactions I was having.

"It would progress like any other relationship. There would just be some elements that are a little different. And we'll bring those in as it seems worthwhile. I can't give you a blueprint, like I said. Each relationship is different."

"I'm not very good at relationships."

His gaze searched my face for a long moment, his expression open and gentle. "I know. Well, really, I think you're not sure whether you're good at them or not. But that's all right. We'll make this into whatever it needs to be for both of us." He took my hands. "You're okay?"

I nodded, afraid to speak. I didn't trust my tongue not to refuse. Sometimes, all you can do is *not* talk.

He leaned forward very slowly, glancing at my lips before looking in my eyes. I had plenty of time to move. It felt like an ice age passed as I watched his lips come closer, watched his eyes search mine. He stopped, just a breath away.

"Kiss me," he said.

I had thought to stay passive. That was how it worked, right? And when his words tumbled over me, I took a moment to understand.

"Caly."

I blinked very quickly, as if it was my vision that needed to be cleared, rather than my mind.

"Kiss me."

When my lips touched his, a shock bolted through me with such intensity, I was afraid my knees would buckle. But within a second, Evan's arms were around me, one hand cradling my neck.

His kiss was gentle, sweet—both in temperament and taste. It was as if we were melding together. When his lips opened, I opened mine in response. His tongue, hot and slick, moved against mine like a lover. I moaned into his mouth, and he kissed me harder.

My whole body came alight. I pressed myself against him, my arms on his thick shoulders. I saw stars behind my eyelids—a whole Independence Day show.

He broke the kiss slowly, sensually.

When I opened my eyes, he was staring at me. It wasn't his inquisitive look. Nor his smirky look. He looked at me with a softness in his eyes I'd never quite seen. And then he smiled, his left-side dimple deep and pronounced. "Are you ready?"

I nodded. This seemed very familiar.

"Will you come with me?"

---

In his room, the light on the nightstand cast a soft, warm glow. He guided me beside the bed, my back to the mattress. With Evan being nearly a head taller than me, I had to crane my neck to look at him. He brought both hands up and laid fingertips on my brow. The forefinger of each hand traced the line of each eyebrow, a feather touch. He moved down and traced my cheekbones to my hairline, then to my ears.

The tickle of his fingers along the shells of my ears gave me a shiver, and I closed my eyes. His smell had wrapped around me in a hug, and I breathed in deeply. As he finished with my ears, his palms closed in and rested on either side of my neck. He drew me closer, and his lips grazed mine.

I moved into the kiss, but he leaned away and brushed a thumb over my lips. I kissed his thumb. I waited for him to slide it into my mouth—because that's what a guy would do—but he didn't. Instead, he slid his hands to my shoulders and pushed one of the straps of my dress down.

Cool air kissed my skin, and I opened my eyes. He'd moved back a step and was looking down at me. At my body.

"A woman in a dress where a single strap has slid down her shoulder...that's one of the sexiest things." Now he met my gaze, heat in his eyes. "You're gorgeous."

I'd had men compliment me before but usually for a purpose. And fat girls don't often get told they're gorgeous. Cute, yes. Adorable, yes. Gorgeous? Sexy? Hot? Not as often as you'd think. His gaze was so intent, so focused, and his words so sincere. I blushed and looked at the floor.

He tilted my chin up. "You're not a wilting flower. Stop acting like it." He planted those lips on mine and tore a kiss from me. I couldn't help but respond, pushing my tongue into his mouth.

His hands had moved; he pawed my ass, hiking my dress up. I reached for him and pulled him to me, but he captured my forearms in his hands and moved them behind my back. He broke the kiss and looked into my eyes, that mischievous glint twinkling. "Lie down on the bed. On your back."

He frog-walked me backward until the edge of the mattress bumped my thighs—it was a very tall bed. He released my arms and poked both shoulders with his hands, tipping me. My skirt had stayed bunched up at my waist. He grinned, waggled his eyebrows, and I laughed.

I shifted back on the bed a little so my feet and calves hung off the edge. He moved them apart and stood between them. He eyed my body, black lace panties just visible beneath the hem of my hiked-up skirt.

"Those are very pretty. It's too bad they're not staying around." He leaned forward, slid his hands up my thighs, over my hips, and hooked his fingers in the waistband. I raised myself as he pulled, the cool air again brushing my hot skin.

When my panties were safely discarded, he spread my legs farther apart, had me bend them at the knees, and settled in between them, his face directly over my pussy.

"Not waxed."

"No."

"But it's trimmed up very nicely."

"Can you believe I've never had my pussy-grooming regime critiqued?"

He laughed and air rolled hot against my skin. "I'm not critiquing. I'm observing." He ran his fingers through the tuft of hair on my mons.

I was successful in keeping myself from jerking my hips up. Barely.

"I like it," he said.

"Oh good. Because my life was hinging on whether you liked it or not."

He looked up my body at me, an eyebrow raised. "There's a nice mouth you've got on you."

"You told me I wasn't a wilting flower, remember?"

"Guilty. Let's see if we can get that mouth to make different sounds."

He dipped his head, and the soft wetness of the tip of his tongue slid along the cleft of my lips. He didn't part them, just teased along the edge, sending ripples through me. I sucked in a breath.

"Yes," he said. "That's a much better sound."

He took another swipe at my pussy, this time barely parting the lips. His tongue brushed against the hood of my clit and sent a flash straight through me. I jerked my hips. I couldn't help it. He ran one hand lightly along the skin of my thigh, adding more sensation.

His fingers moved to my pussy lips, and he spread them open. The air cooled the wet skin, and I shivered again, though not really from the temperature. My whole body tingled, and I wanted, more than anything, his mouth on me.

"Please," I whispered. I didn't even know whether it was loud enough for him to hear me.

His tongue ran a path from my entrance to my clit...once, twice, and a third time. On the third, he moved from right to left over my clit and hood. It sent shocks through all my limbs. Heat ricocheted beneath my skin. My nipples rubbed almost painfully against the fabric of my bra. I pulled the cups down, freeing them, because the sensation was too much. I was already getting overloaded.

Evan slid a fingertip inside me—just the tip—and while he continued to lick my clit back and forth, he moved his fingertip up and down just in my entrance. Everything in me responded. I felt that flip of the switch inside—one that told me that this more than just felt good. That if it continued, I would barrel straight into a huge orgasm. Heat gathered in my belly. I realized I'd been grinding my hips. I didn't know for how long. I didn't really care.

Suddenly, his tongue was gone, and his finger stilled. I groaned out my frustration. I looked down my body to see him watching me, his lips glistening with my juices.

"Not until I say, Caly." He paused. "You understand?"

I nodded, and he lowered his head again. I counted the seconds until his tongue was on me. One. Two. Three. Four. "Oh!"

His tongue was inside, and his thumb on my clit. He flicked his tongue up and down inside me, while his thumb moved in slow circles. A wave rolled through me—not an orgasm, but tingles, electric pulses, feelings I couldn't even name. I rode the wave as it built higher and higher.

"God... I can't..."

His tongue slid out of me. "Wait." And back in. He never stopped giving my clit attention. Not for a second.

Somehow his word made it both harder and easier. Easier, because I had to control it; I *had* to hold on. Harder, because his order stabbed straight to the base of that wave I was riding and made it so close to cresting.

Then he switched again, his tongue on my clit, back and forth, back and forth. There had been a split second where I could breathe, but only a second. His finger slid into me again, flicking up and down just inside, rubbing all the nerve endings, and that wave...it got impossibly higher, peaking...

"I can't...please!"

"Hold it."

A breath before he started back on my clit. I squeezed my eyes shut, little white pulses shooting off behind my lids. I whimpered.

Evan's tongue moved faster, and the sparks flipping through me weren't going to stop this time; I just knew it.

"Please, please, please! It's coming. I can't hold back."

"Ask me."

I didn't even think about it. It was all I could do to speak and hold my orgasm at bay at the same time. "Can I come, please?" He didn't say anything, his tongue back on that spot. "Please? Please?"

"Come for me."

I finally released the hold against that wave, and it crested and crashed over me. My entire body untensed for half a second before my muscles contracted and my orgasm rolled through me. It started as tightness and electricity in my pussy that shot through my body all the way to the tips of my toes and fingers. I cried out; I know I did. It wasn't coherent because I wasn't coherent. It was only the pleasure—the high, intense, muscle-binding pleasure.

Evan kept his movements up, but slowed them as the orgasm tapered out. Finally, his tongue on my clit became too much, and I squirmed, pressing a hand against his head to push him away.

He didn't budge. His tongue stopped moving though, as well as his finger. But he didn't move them away. Now his tongue just pressed my clit. I felt the little bud pulse against it. Actually, I felt the pulse everywhere. My whole body was my heartbeat.

My breath came in long, heavy pants and I couldn't even open my eyes. I felt like a big pile of goo. I scritched at his head, trying to show my appreciation.

"I'm not done yet," he said. Cool air skimmed over my pussy. It occurred to me I might have soaked the bed, but I couldn't bring myself to care much.

"I'm good for now."

Evan chuckled. "That has no bearing on it."

I jerked my eyes open and looked at him. The twinkle. The grin. And then he disentangled himself from me, slid open the drawer of the nightstand, and pulled out a small thing. It looked a bit like a spark plug.

I propped myself up on my elbows. "What is that?"

He only grinned and settled back between my legs. He twisted the base of the thing, and it let out a strong, constant buzz.

"Oooh."

I wasn't sure whether the grin could look more mischievous, but I imagined it did. He set the business end of the little vibrator against the top of my mound, just above my clit. The vibrations traveled along the lips, making everything feel tingly. He ran it down one lip, across, and up the other.

I dropped back on the bed and felt my pussy gush. Evan circled near all the sensitive areas but never touched the vibrator to my clit, never entered my pussy. It didn't take long before I was rotating my hips desperately, trying to get it where I wanted it to go. The coolness of the air told me my pussy was open and exposed.

A throaty chuckle and his voice came out husky. "You look so sexy writhing around there. Hot. Wanting."

I couldn't even care enough to blush at what I must look like. When he removed the toy and then made it hover directly over my clit, I almost wanted to cry. The tiniest of vibrations tickled the skin. It was like only a pinpoint of the vibrator touched me. I arched my hips up, and he eased back.

"Ahhh! Evan! Please. God."

He moved the vibrator close again, touching just a tiny bit more. The tingles started again. I felt them building in my pussy, rippling out. Evan made a little more contact, and then my entire body shook as the orgasm rose faster than I'd expected.

And then the vibrator was gone. I wanted to scream.

"Evan!"

He chuckled again and slid off the bed. Again, into the nightstand drawer, this time, he drew out a condom and ripped the packet open with his teeth. He set the vibrator—still going—on the crook where my leg met my torso, sending delicious little feelings along my skin, almost to where it would get me off. Almost.

As I reached for the toy, Evan said, "Don't touch it."

I wrinkled my nose at him, and he grinned. But I moved my hand away, wondering if I could wiggle the toy to where I wanted.

After he put the condom on, he stood at the side of the bed. He leaned forward, wrapped his thick arms around my thighs and pulled me bodily to the edge of the bed.

I think I've mentioned that I'm a bit of a big girl. I realized just then how strong he was.

He grabbed the vibe and hiked my legs up. The head of his cock just nudged my entrance.

"You're so wet. Look at that." And he did. He stared down at our almost-joining, his hands holding my calves up and wide, the vibe in his hand, pressed against my skin, still on and vibrating against my calf muscle. Then he shifted his gaze to mine.

We stared at each other as he slowly—it felt like a centimeter at a time—pushed his cock into me. I felt every movement, felt every bit being stretched as he entered. His gaze held me to him more tightly than his hands.

He stopped just before he was seated. A long pause sat in the air. My whole body was ready. I wanted him. I wanted everything.

His gaze searched my face, and then he slammed home, rocking my entire body. He filled me hard, and the shock vibrated up my whole torso, my spine, through every cell. I gasped as he released my legs and leaned down against me. His lips sought out mine, and he captured my tongue in his mouth. I devoured him as much as he did me.

He eased back enough to pull out an inch or two, putting space between our torsos. His hand came around— I'd forgotten about the vibrator. He slid his hand between us and lay the vibrator along my slit, business end pressed against my clit. It sent delicious heat through me. He dropped onto me, elbows holding him up on either side. The vibe made my entire pussy alive. I felt its throb through every inch of skin.

Then he angled backward with his hips and slammed into me again. And then again. The vibe rubbed along my slick lips with each of his thrusts. His cock filled me over and over again. That wave was back—it was an entire beach full of them.

"You're going to come for me," Evan said, his voice soft but firm, husky. "I'm going to count backward from five and when I get to zero, you're going to come. You understand, Caly?" He never stopped pumping me. Never paused in filling me with his cock.

"Y-yes. Please...hurry."

A distracted chuckle. But he didn't count. He leaned his head down and nipped at the round swell of my breast. He pushed it up with a hand and sucked the nipple into his mouth. Electric jolts shot between my pussy and my nipple.

"Evan!" I wasn't going to be able to hold it off. There was no way.

"Five," he said, his voice muffled.

I almost cried with relief. The vibrator had nudged itself right beside my clit—right where my sweetest spot was. "Please...please hurry." He plundered me with his cock, and I knew there was no way I was going to make it. No way.

He released my nipple and looked at me. I arched my neck, trying to tense all my muscles so I wouldn't come. Guys say reciting baseball stats will keep a person from coming. I don't know baseball stats, but multiplication tables were doing nothing.

"Four."

I panted. My pulse pounded in my ears. He crushed me under him and sweat dripped on my chest.

"Three."

*Hurry, hurry, hurry.* It was a mantra in my head. I pushed the orgasm away. I tried so hard. His entire body scraped against me, and I imagined I could feel every hair. I clung to his shoulders, his biceps.

"Two."

I let out a small, strangled cry. I wasn't going to make it. I wanted to. I wanted to so badly. The vibe had started rolling back and forth over my clit. Evan shifted his angle only slightly, and now his cock was hitting a spot inside me that made the pleasure a million times stronger. "Oh God, oh God, oh God, oh God."

"One. Not yet."

I closed my eyes, everything in me just focusing on his sounds. His breathing. The occasional grunt. The next word that came out of him was going to be my undoing. And I waited for it. I held my breath and waited.

He lowered himself, slid his hands beneath my arms and curled them over my shoulders. I wrapped my arms over his. His breath puffed against my ear.

"Zero." His voice, so soft, so strong. "Come for me."

I let out a desperate little sound, like a mewl, as I finally let go of my self-control. He pounded into me, and I yelled out his name as everything—all the sensations I'd felt since this started—*everything* crashed through me. I spiraled out of control, heat flashing through every cell. I held on to him, clawed at him, clutched him. I rode out my orgasm as Evan held me tight.

He sped up, slamming into me, then growled low in his throat and made one hard thrust. I felt that thrust up to the top of my head. And another thrust, this one not as hard. A fierce growl. And one last thrust as the rumble subsided.

I all but collapsed, every muscle a quivering, ridiculous mess.

He still held me tight, his body covered in sweat. He shifted his hips a little, which made the vibrator—still running—lie right over my clit.

"Oh! Ow! No, no. Get off, please."

I squirmed around beneath him, and he hiked himself up and stared at me, looking confused.

"The vibrator. Too sensitive. Please." No coherent sentences for me.

He laughed and rolled off. I swatted the thing away and released a big breath.

"Poor girl. Too many orgasms. Too sensitive."

I wrinkled my nose at him. I debated swatting him too but then decided I didn't have the energy. Swatting a vibrator was draining, apparently.

Evan picked up the offending little toy and switched it off. He laid it on the nightstand and then stood. "I'll be right back." He moved toward the bathroom.

I thought about getting up, following him in, and molesting him in the shower. But my muscles were not as yet under my control. So I just lay there. When he returned, he paused at the side of the bed, looking at me.

"You look beautifully fucked."

"I have definitely been beautifully fucked."

"Not so bad," he said as he sat on the edge of the bed, facing me, "this control thing, right?" His expression said he already knew my answer.

"That not coming isn't easy, you know. You should try it some time!"

He raised both brows and then laughed. "Yes, I know. Men don't ever try not to come when they're fucking a woman."

I pulled myself up onto my elbows. "Well, I am not convinced that most try to hold off."

"I think we can debate other men at a different time. What do you think?"

I nodded and tilted myself up into a sitting position. I needed to pee. Suddenly and very urgently. I shimmied past him, off the bed. "Excuse me. My turn." I heard his chuckle as I closed the door.

# Epilogue

"Oooof. Do you have to pull it that tight? Can't…breathe." I held on to the door frame as Evan pulled a set of laces behind me. My entire torso was encased in brocade and steel boning.

"Don't be melodramatic, woman. You're fine."

"Are you sure this is dress code? I mean, you're not all dolled up in medieval torture devices."

"This isn't a torture device. Don't fret. When we get there, you'll understand how this isn't one of those." He stopped tugging on the laces, and I felt him tying them off. "Are you nervous?" He patted my backside when he'd finished.

I turned and faced him. He looked pretty fucking fine in his suit. It was a full three piece—vest and everything. Charcoal gray, dark tie, silver vest. I was about ready to jump him. Again. "Yes. I'm not sure what to expect."

"Don't worry." He went into the closet, and his words got muffled. "You'll be with me. No one would bother you anyway, even if you were there on your own." He emerged with a pair of dark red satin pumps and handed them to me. "It's not like you have to do anything. You could just stand and watch."

"Do a lot of people do that? Just watch?" I sat on the edge of the bed and then realized corsets don't allow much in the way of bending over. My boobs were just about strangling me.

"Some." He leaned against the dresser and watched me with crossed arms and an annoying grin. I eventually held the shoes by their backs and slid my toes in.

"Somehow I have this idea of dungeons and play parties as being all-out beat-and-fuck orgies."

He laughed the full-throated laugh that I'd come to love. Yeah, I used the word. It came more easily these days.

"I suppose some could be that. This party won't be, though. You will likely see beating and some fucking—"

"And rope?"

His eyes twinkled. "And rope, yes. But it's not a free-for-all. There won't be a pile of writhing bodies in the middle of the floor."

"Good. I don't think I'm ready for that." I stood and held my arms out wide. "How do I look?" I did a little twirl.

"Gorgeous. I may have to beat people off with sticks."

"That would just blend in, right?"

He laughed again and gestured me to the bedroom door. I went through, he followed, and we went out to the living room. When I'd moved in last month, Evan had said I was welcome to make some changes to the decor, but I hadn't done much aside from a couple oversize throw pillows, a shelf of books—with extra space for mine, due out next year—and some framed photos of people I love. Evan had good taste, and his living room felt safe—like home.

He retrieved coats from the closet—it had been an unseasonably cool October—draped his over a chair, and held mine out for me. As I slid my arms into it, I asked, "Are you doing to...do anything with me tonight?"

As he pushed the coat onto my shoulders, he kissed my ear. "Perhaps."

I spun around. "Are you serious?"

He laughed. "No. I likely won't do anything to you in public this time. It being your first foray out, after all. But next time..." He shrugged into his coat and took my hand. "Don't worry. You'll be fine. This is just another part of the game."

I turned so that I was square in front of him. "I love your game." I quirked up a corner of my mouth.

He leaned in, his sweet scent washing over me and making my belly flip. He brushed his lips against mine. "And I love you."

*The End*

Did you like what you read? Please be sure to go back to the online retailer of your choice and leave a review! Reviews are how authors get readers. The more good word of mouth about the book, the better it is for the author! So leave reviews for all the authors you love! ☺

Interested in what happens next? Caly and Evan's adventures will continue in the first installment of the short story series, *Sanctum Shorts*. Check out the sneak peek on the next page!

Want to know when it's going to come out? Hop into my Sexy Sheets and get notification when new stories come out!

http://www.trinitywrites.com/trinitys-sexy-sheets/

## *Sneak Peek*

*Sanctum Shorts: Are You Willing?*

*Please note: This Sneak Peek is not a final version. The published edition may contain minor changes.*

My phone buzzed in the pocket of my cargo shorts. I swiped a forearm over my sweaty forehead and pulled off my work glove.

Evan: I'll be back at my apartment around 6, enough time for a shower before we head out to dinner.

Before I'd even finished typing "Okay," he'd sent another.

Evan: I've left clothes out on my bed for you, along with a couple other things. Be sure you're ready when I get home.

My breath caught for a second and then poofed out in a tiny cloud in front of my face. Little pinpricks of desire tingled in my belly. I backspaced over my "Okay."

Me: Yes sir.

I spent the rest of my volunteer time at Helping Hands, the homeless shelter I spent most weekends at, completely distracted. Luckily, for this shift, I was on the team tasked with cleaning up the back garden and yard area, so I was pulling weeds and relocating mulch. No need for brain power or focus. Or interacting with other people, especially Annette, who had a nose for … well, everything.

Evan and I had met when he'd designed the new building for Helping Hands that I'd spearheaded funding for. And Annette, co-owner of the shelter along with her partner, Jessie, had spent the three months since we'd started dating trying to guess at where we were, how committed we'd become. I suspected that she would be taken a little aback if she learned the exact nature of our relationship.

The thought of how I'd explain having been in a dungeon the night before made me laugh. One of the other volunteers, Debra, glanced over and I waved, before yanking another weed from the bed. She waved back.

I wasn't really sure how to explain to myself what being in a dungeon was like. I'd met a lot of very nice people — only two of whom I remember their names — but the atmosphere was like nowhere I'd ever been. People walked around in states of undress and their comfort at that made me comfortable with it. It was like it was normal. I supposed it was.

I wasn't going to be getting naked any time soon though. I tossed a pile of pulled weeds into the wheelbarrow between Olive and me. I didn't care what Evan said.

Caly is not running around naked at Sanctum. Nope. Not gonna happen.

Then I thought about Evan's texts. My skin heated up and my hand froze mid-way to pulling out another clump.

What if he wanted me to get naked *tonight*? What if that's what him choosing my clothes meant?

I couldn't work out how that made me feel. I mean, terrified, definitely. But there was something else. Something hot.

I didn't want to think about it, so I pushed it away. But the thoughts tumbled in the back of my head for the rest of the afternoon. By the time I left at four thirty, I was a ridiculous, turned-on mess.

---

I let myself into Evan's house through the back door. I'd already stopped home and showered — nothing like my own toiletries to help me relax. Now there was just the matter of the clothes he wanted me to wear.

I'd been kind of obsessing about it since I'd left Helping Hands — whether he was picking out the clothes so that he could take them off me there.

What if he wanted to fuck me at Sanctum? I didn't remember seeing that sex was against the rules, though I hadn't seen anyone fucking there the night before. It all seemed so strange, so foreign.

I took a deep breath. His kitchen had a perpetual smell of pasta sauce and garlic. It was a scent I associated with Evan as much as I associated him with the sweet, spicy smell of his skin. I let the breathing and the lovely scent slow my heart.

"Get it together, Caly," I told myself. "Just chill out."

I passed through the living room, where we'd had our first rope scene, before we'd even kissed. Thinking about that, about the sensual feel of his hands and the rope on my skin... the way he'd pulled me back against him... his heat, his touch...

I blew out a breath. If I wasn't careful, I was going to have to go rub one out right now. And that would probably not going to earn me points with Evan. I laughed at myself.

I made my way to the end of the hall. The van's bedroom, with the blinds closed, sat shrouded in shadows. I chased them away with a flick of the light switch.

On the neatly made, king size bed lay a simple and elegant dress in midnight blue. It would probably fall just above the knees and the neckline, while a little deep, wasn't bad enough to be mistaken for a hooker. I liked that Evan had somewhat modest tastes.

Especially if he was going to be dressing *me*. I gave myself a smirk.

Beside the dress lay undergarments.

One of the first things Evan had done when I'd agreed to try a relationship based in dominance and submission was get all my measurements. Like, *everything*. And he would randomly buy me clothes that always seemed to fit perfectly. It could be a bit astounding, how easily he seemed to find beautiful things for me. Especially considering that designers often took smaller sizes and just made them bigger, apparently not even thinking that they sit on different bodies...well, differently.

So Evan's ability to find things that looked good on me all on his own was pretty impressive. I didn't think tonight would be any different.

Stockings, with Cuban heels — Evan's favorite — along with a simple black garter belt. And beside those... a lush, emerald green lace demi bra and panty set. It was stunning. And the panties. I laughed. Evan knew I loved boyshorts. So the matching panties were gorgeous, lacy boyshorts. A pair of simple, satin, black heels sat on the floor, their toes snugged just under the bed.

Just beside the panties lay a simple black clutch purse with a folded piece of paper on top. I unfolded the note.

*Caly,*

*Please shower and dress in the clothing I've provided. I will get home at 6. Be sitting on my side of the bed, facing the door, when I arrive.*

*I very much look forward to seeing you. It is going to be a lovely evening.*

*Evan*

I had the surreal feeling of my stomach being both at my feet and in my throat. My nerve endings jangled with desire and I realized suddenly that I was wet. Drenched, even. I wondered, in passing, if I was going to need to take another shower.

I set the note down carefully and then went about getting ready.

---

*Are You Willing* is already out! You can find all my published books on my website:

http://www.trinitywrites.com/books

---

Want to know when other Sanctum novels and Shorts will be released? Hop into my Sexy Sheets and get notification when new stories come out!

http://www.trinitywrites.com/trinitys-sexy-sheets/

# Trinity

Trinity writes realistic kink! Trinity came up in the Atlanta BDSM scene in the mid-90s and has been an active kink and poly person for two decades. She's traveled the Southeast, from the Carolinas to Louisiana, teaching classes about kink and D/s. Her particular passions are service, ritual, and rope, which readers will see reflected in her work. And, of course, hot sex!

In 2008, Trinity entered the publishing industry in an editorial capacity. She's taught writing classes at numerous conventions and private writing events, and she edits freelance for many genres—romance to horror. She thrives on helping other writers improve their craft.

Now, Trinity combines her two obsess—err…passions by writing hot, sexy kink stories! It's important to her that her work resonates especially with those who know and understand the kink and poly lifestyles. If it's accurate to those who "get it," then it will be most helpful for those just learning it. That's not to say Trinity won't write stories without BDSM. Variety is what makes life spicy! But you can count on her to bring you great, realistic kink. Follow her on Twitter: @Trinity_writes and even catch her live on Periscope:@Trinity_writes.